MORALLY GREY

LAUREN BIEL

Library of Congress Cataloging-in-Publication Data

Morally Grey/Lauren Biel 1st ed.

Cover Design: Laura Hidalgo @Spellbinding Design

Editing: Sugar Free Editing

Interior Design: Sugar Free Editing

For more information on this book and the author, visit: www.LaurenBiel.com

Please visit LaurenBiel.com for a full list of content warnings.

This one's for the girls who drool over mugshots

Chapter One

Grey

This moment doesn't feel real. Even as I step onto the sidewalk, even as the tangible earth rushes up to meet each of my solid footfalls, I feel very outside of myself. That's to be expected, I suppose. I lost a piece of my soul the day my wife died, and a year of anguish hasn't lessened that loss of connection. Feeling very outside of myself is nothing new.

I glance down at my watch as I finger the cold metal tucked inside my waistband. It's just after five in the evening, and the lady of the hour should appear at any moment. The human part of me says this is wrong. What I plan to do goes against everything we're taught from an early age.

But this bitch ruined my life.

A woman emerges from the building and heads toward the back parking lot, but she isn't my target. She's a cog in their machine, but she doesn't press the buttons. My issue lies with the button mashers.

It doesn't have to be this way. Before I settled on the finality of murder, I considered other avenues. With my background in computer sciences, hacking into her home security system and learning her dirty secrets wasn't very difficult. My plan was to wipe her accounts and leave her high and dry, but then I discovered just how vile some of her secrets truly are.

Like the way she neglects the two adopted children in her care. Or perhaps people would like to hear the racial slurs she slings about her staff and clients. And don't even get me started on the many "charities" she donates to. The real ones have yet to see a dime, and her house of cards isn't long for this world.

But justice just isn't swift enough for me. Justice isn't revenge.

And I want revenge.

The gun's metal burns against my skin in an ominous reminder of the level of desperation I've succumbed to. The cold fire reminds me that there's no other option. She needs to die.

Minutes feel like hours, and another ten minutes pass before the bank door opens and closes. The blonde woman turns to lock the door with her chain of keys. After killing her, I could easily snatch those keys and take every penny from inside that bank, but I don't want the money anymore. I just want the house I lost. I want my wife and child to be alive again. Money hardly has importance to me any longer, and since it made this woman selfish enough to screw over who knows how many families, it holds even less value for me now.

The only thing that can right the world is for her to die like my wife, but that isn't possible. My wife died a slow, agonizing death. She endured fear and pain before finally bleeding out. I'll just have to settle for the next best thing and give her a quick death.

But a death, nonetheless.

I'll remove her from this world. I'll take her away from her massive home, no doubt built on the backs of desperate people like me. Has she ever received those terrifying letters with a red Past Due written across the top? I guarantee she never had to eat, sleep, and shit on the street. I'm certain she hasn't watched someone die a painful death that she herself set in motion.

Studies show that the rate of suicides related to foreclosures *doubled* during the housing crisis. *All* of those deaths, including my wife's and child's, are on her hands. Her hands and every single bank CEO who put their greed above the lives of their clients.

Over my life. Over Sarah and the baby I didn't even have the heart to name without his mother.

I've had time to get over this, to let it all go, but the passage of time didn't heal my wounds. The anger brewed, bubbled, and boiled inside me, growing hotter by the day. The worst part, though? The burn just keeps burning. Keeps searing me and making me hope for death. It will never end.

I rub the pistol's grip before I pull it out of my waistband. I have looked down this barrel so many times and talked myself down from the ultimate end. The chance to see my wife and son again. But I swear I heard her voice telling me no, that I couldn't leave this world until Gloria Rogers is dead.

After scanning the area, I step out from the alley and begin to follow her. I grip my pistol beneath the right flap of my jacket.

"Gloria!" I call out. My voice nearly startles me as it shatters the silence.

The blonde turns to look at me. She doesn't even recognize me. She doesn't remember selling me a fucking pipe dream. The woman is willfully blind to the damage she's done.

I had a whole speech planned out for when I came face to face with her. I planned to tell her how her greed has ruined the lives of so many. But just seeing her beady brown eyes makes my throat tighten. Her nose rises a few inches as she looks annoyed at me for wasting her time, and I can't speak.

I pull the gun into the light. Fuck speeches. Fuck explaining my loss to a woman who wouldn't care. She only cares about her life now, not anyone else's.

She squeals and throws her purse at my feet. I don't deserve to feel fucking offended, but I do. I know what I look like. Rough around the edges. Stubble lining my jaw. Dark, messy hair that hasn't been washed in nearly a week. My eyes are probably bloodshot from lack of sleep, but she sees an addict. An addict who wants what she has.

If she only knew what I want from her. And what she'll be forced to give me. If she only knew the only thing I'm addicted to is my desire to see her die at my hand.

I step around her bougie bag and cock the hammer. "This isn't a robbery, lady. This is revenge."

Her mouth opens as she draws a breath, likely to scream for help, but my finger pulls back on the trigger before she utters a sound. Noise erupts from the gun's barrel in a flash of light, and the woman crumples in a heap of designer fabric. Her legs shuffle around, knocking off one of her expensive heels, and then she stills.

Blood pools beneath her. It isn't like you see in the

movies, however. It isn't a fast-moving river, and it's mildly disappointing. I do feel powerful, though. Vindicated. As if I've taken back some of my control.

I tuck the gun inside my pants and run, ignoring the muzzle's heat pressed against my lower abdomen. As I hurry from the scene and slip into an alleyway, I pull clothes from my backpack and throw a zip-up over my shirt, then zip it to hide the evidence of my crime.

Seconds later, sirens blare from the main street, and I slink away before anyone notices me. At least, I *hope* no one noticed me. I didn't exactly think this far ahead. I wasn't even sure I could complete the task.

But now that I have, that leaves me with one very important question. Where the fuck do I hide?

Chapter Two

Briar

The trudge to my car after work has never seemed longer. I swear the pavement stretches by a few inches each day. Sliding into the driver's seat, I take a deep breath and try to relax the tension crammed inside my shoulders.

My job isn't easy. I spend the entire day telling patients they can't afford their life-saving surgery. We really are living the American dream, aren't we? The few minutes with the radio blaring at the end of the day is my way of trying to decompress. It's my attempt at forgetting all the tears that were shed today, all the pleading words uttered from terrified lips.

When I feel a little less shitty, I start the car and head home, but as I pull into my driveway, I dread my trip to the mailbox. I know what will be waiting for me in that innocuous white box. A statement that will let me know I'm overdue on several bills. I'll end up tossing the letter on the mountain of debt I won't be able to pay. The cost of living continues to increase, but my employers aren't paying me more.

Debt is genetic for me. My parents were in massive debt for most of my childhood. We almost lost our home on numerous occasions. No matter how much they worked, they couldn't get ahead of it. Inability must be hereditary. Or maybe it's stupidity. Either way, this shit is generational.

A shiver rides up my spine at the thought of my father. We didn't lose the house, but that was only because he paid one bank with the money he stole from another. Yes, he robbed a bank. It was wrong and inherently terrible, but ending up in the streets seemed worse. Desperation drives people to do terrible, unthinkable things. Like walking into a bank with a gun and a dream.

Forcing the thoughts from my head, I ignore the mailbox for now and head straight for the fridge. I didn't have time for lunch today, so I'm starving. I grab a box of leftover pasta and head to the couch.

They'll probably cut my cable due to non-payment soon, so I lift the remote and flick through some channels while I still can. I pick up a cold glob of noodles and shove it into my mouth. While scanning channels, I stop at the local news station as they show a scene of genuine chaos. A reporter talks into a camera as a few cops mill around behind her, looking down at what appears to be a pool of blood.

A red banner runs along the bottom of the screen. I swallow a bite of food and read it aloud. "Bank CEO assassinated," I whisper. They even show a clip of the masked man outside the bank, standing and waiting for the woman to emerge. She tosses her purse at his feet, but he doesn't grab it.

Odd.

Intrigued, I lower the remote and keep watching, and the news anchor confirms my suspicions. He never took her purse. Didn't even touch it. So if his motive wasn't robbery . . .

A picture of a smiling, professional woman appears on the screen. Blonde hair curtains her head, and her teeth probably cost more than everything I own combined. I grab my phone and immediately Google her name. She looks nice enough. A single woman raising adopted children on her own doesn't seem like the typical target for a hit, especially if robbery wasn't a factor. So . . . why'd he do it?

There has to be a reason. If it wasn't financial gain, was it a lover's quarrel? Did she hurt him in some way? Are the adopted children his relatives and he would like to regain custody?

That's when the suspect's image flashes across the screen again. Bright blue eyes peer at the camera through the gap in a black balaclava. A few strands of dark hair poke from beneath the hood and touch his eyebrows.

Seconds later, another image replaces this one. It shows the "person of interest" inside a gas station an hour before the crime. He doesn't look like someone who would kill a woman for no reason. Sure, he looks a bit rough, like he's been sleeping on the street for a while, but as I scroll to the Facebook page of our local news station, I have to agree with the hundreds of women who have already left comments beneath his picture.

He's fucking hot.

As I continue scrolling, I make up stories in my mind about why the masked vigilante did what he did. I imagine his family shivering in a box on the fucking street because he lost all they owned. I can almost feel his hatred toward the CEO who signed off on the predatory practices. A blazing fire lights inside me, and that animosity worms through my body.

Because it could have been my father. He was nearly pushed to take a human life. All because of corporate greed.

But I'll probably never know why this particular man did what he did. He's a ghost in the wind, and I hope no one reports him. Whoever this man is, he might be a hero. Even if he's a murderer.

I turn off the television and try to get on with the rest of my evening. After finishing off the pasta, I toss the takeout box into the trash and head for my bathroom. But even the shower can't clear my mind. I can't get his face out of my head. The masked killer consumes my every waking thought.

What is he doing now? Is he hiding out somewhere? Did he run away and possibly hurt himself? I've created several scenarios in my mind, and I'm living in a fantasy world at this point. I imagine what I'd do if I saw him. The reward money is tempting—and bound to rise with each day that passes. I do have a lot of bills to pay . . .

Listen, I know it's my fault. I was the one who ran up the cards and spent far more than I could afford. But that's the game, isn't it? They're banking on the people who can't pay those interest fees. They're betting on the people who will buy into the dream they can't afford.

For their entire fucking lifetimes.

It's a shitty setup, but it's also been around for ages and isn't likely to change anytime soon. Maybe the hot guy had some major debt too. I could see how those constantly rising bills could bring someone to the brink of insanity. We're all inching closer to the edge, aren't we?

But he didn't take the money . . .

Stepping out of the shower, I dry myself off and try to

push the image of his face from my mind. I shouldn't be this attracted to a killer. He took another person's life in cold blood. I can joke around and pretend that I understand, but I don't. Not really.

My father understood it, though. That's why he put his life on the line and robbed a bank. When his back was against the wall and the bill collectors came knocking, he didn't cower in fear. He stood up and opened the door. I knew my father's actions were wrong, but in my eyes, he was a hero. After all, isn't that what heroes do? They save people who are drowning, and we were definitely drowning.

In the eyes of the law, however, he was no hero. He was just a thief.

That brings me back around to the question of *why*. My father's motive was clear enough. He stole money to help his family. But why did this vigilante need to steal a life? It wasn't for financial gain, since he didn't take the woman's purse, so what did he get out of it?

Without realizing it, I've taken a seat in front of my computer and pulled up the articles about him. Each one says the same thing, that they don't know who he is or why he's committed the crime. They're written with the same verbiage, as if they were all typed by the same hand and gifted to the national news agencies.

Yet I read each one. I study the same pictures.

Like a gluttonous woman, I sit at my desk and feast on the same sustenance, over and over, and still I'm not satisfied. I print out the pictures and paste them to a bit of purple cardstock. There are only three images for now. The one where he wears the balaclava, another where he's at the gas station, and a third from just after the crime that shows him slipping into a back alley.

My hands move on autopilot as I reach for my sketch-book and my trusty HB pencil. Studying his features, I begin mapping his face on the paper. I start with the shape of his head, focusing on the sharp cut of his jaw. The pencil scrapes along the page, forming his lips, his blue eyes, his straight smile.

A perfect killer.

With the sketch in place, I start a pot of coffee. I should be asleep right now, prepping for another long shift at the hospital, but I've found a muse. The urge to draw him and capture his details on paper overwhelms me.

After plopping a heaping dose of vanilla cream and sugar into the mug, I settle at my desk again and pull out my detail pencils, a kneaded eraser, and some charcoal. For hours on end, I smudge and shape and erase until his face practically pops off the page.

I glance at the clock. It's nearly three in the morning, and my shift starts in two hours. The thought of returning to the hospital and missing news updates on the murderer makes my skin crawl, so I do what any sensible woman would do. I call in and say that I'm sick. I have some time off saved up, so it won't hurt my bottom line. Though I do feel a little guilty for the others who will have to pick up the slack I leave behind.

But only a little.

With that settled, I place my drawing beside the photos. It's beginning to look like a proper shrine, which is a bit creepy, but it's not like anyone will see it. I don't exactly entertain visitors on a regular basis. The girls and guys at work like me well enough, but I'm in exactly zero inner circles.

I shuffle to the couch and lie down, in direct view of my new shrine. And as I look at his pictures, I fall asleep.

Chapter Three

Grey

The murder weapon burns my skin despite the barrel's cool temperature. I need to get rid of it, I know that, but every time I try to let it go, it feels . . . wrong. Each time I find a new spot, I fear it's too obvious, too close to a camera or something. The cops already tagged my full face in a gas station video, and I can't risk another fuckup.

A cop is heading my way, so I turn my face to avoid him seeing me. No one notices anyone in the city. Even when looking for a murderer, it seems. I raise my hood and walk the last block to my car.

I parked a mile away from the scene because I couldn't risk the added cameras. I knew this area didn't have any. After spending the night in a filthy alley, I'm ready to get back to safety, and my car is the best I have. As the morning sun bursts between the buildings, I slide behind the steering wheel, and the endorphins in my brain die when the gravity of what I've done pushes me into the seat.

I killed a person.

I fucking killed her.

But my guilt takes a back seat as a cop car flashes its lights behind me in the parking lot. I peer into the rearview mirror and curl my fingers around the gun. Shooting a cop wasn't on my bingo card, though, so I release my hold on the weapon. No one else needs to die.

Then the car swerves around me, and the siren kicks on as he peels out of the parking lot. I live to see another day.

Not that it matters. Now that I've killed the greedy bitch, what purpose does my life have? I live in my fucking car. The life I built, the life I was *building*, went into the ground with my wife and child. I have nothing to lose because I have nothing.

I start the car and pull onto the main road. I need to get out of the heart of the city. The outskirts will be safer. Maybe I can find an abandoned house to sleep in. If I'm discovered, it could bring more heat my way, but I'm already in the fire. I jumped from the frying pan the moment I pulled the trigger and killed the greedy bitch.

The buildings eventually break apart, stretching out until there's space for trees and grass between them instead of concrete and brick. Because the road is so empty out here, I notice when a car approaches behind me. It's a dark SUV, and I'm pretty sure it's an unmarked car.

A side street appears to my right, and I take it. If the SUV makes the turn, I'll know. And sure enough, seconds later, the black behemoth makes the same right. I'm being followed.

Call it paranoia if you must. Actually, that's probably exactly what it is, but why is that a bad thing? Paranoia is just a natural stress response, and I'm fucking stressed. I take the next left and hold my breath.

The SUV takes the same turn.

I'm a rat in a maze, and I've run myself into a dead end. The road leads to a driveway that winds into the woods. If I try to turn around now, my tail will have me cornered. The only thing to do is keep driving.

So I do. As if I belong here, I pull down the driveway and watch my rearview mirror. The black SUV shrinks as it turns around and disappears, but I keep driving until the driveway ends.

Ahead of me stands a small house. It's just a little single-story number, with a shallow front porch and a serious weed problem. There aren't any cars in the driveway, so maybe it's safe if I have a look around. I've already committed murder. What's another charge?

I ease the car to a stop near the garage. The massive door is closed, meaning the homeowners could definitely be inside, but this is a risk I'll have to take. I haven't eaten anything in days, and I can't keep going like this.

This far out in the sticks, there's every chance that whoever lives here hasn't even heard about what I've done. I haven't owned a cell phone in a while, but I remember social media. If murder isn't the flavor of the week, my rebellious act might get buried beneath stories of plane crashes and missing pets. There's always a chance.

And I'm going to take it.

I step out of the car and start toward the front door. A small statue stares up at me as I pass a narrow strip of over-grown earth that was clearly a garden at one point. It's a concrete figure of a small girl holding a watering can, though one of her legs has gone the way of the dodo.

A large window looms above the greenery, and I peer inside. A woman with auburn hair lies on a faded blue couch in her living room. The television blares some morning news program, and I'm sick when my face flashes across the screen, followed by the tale of my misdeed. At least they don't know my name yet. And that's the big word, isn't it? Yet.

I creep around the outside of the house, looking through the windows as I come across them, but she seems to be the only one at home. The single bedroom held no sign of masculinity, so I assume she lives alone.

Overpowering one woman isn't so difficult, especially when I have a weapon. It's a shitty thought to have, but there it is. I've thought it.

But maybe it doesn't have to come to that. Sure, my story was all over the news this morning, but the woman is fast asleep. There's no guarantee she learned about it yesterday. I'll just give her a sob story and hope she buys it. If not, I have the gun.

Clearing my throat, I walk back to the front door and raise my fist to knock. I shuffle my weight between my feet as I wait, but I hear no noise on the other side of the door. After several silent moments, I hurry back to the window. She's still fast asleep on the couch.

Back at the door, I knock a little harder this time. It's too bad she doesn't have a dog or a doorbell. Anything more effective than my fist against wood. But despite my frustration, I'm rewarded with the slide of a lock and an opening door seconds later.

The woman's green eyes blink up at me as she tries to adjust to the land of the living. She's quite pretty, in an unassuming sort of way. Very girl-next-door.

"My car . . . was giving me some trouble, and I think I'm lost anyway. Could I come in and use your phone? I don't own one." I offer her my most genuine and disarming smile and wait for recognition to dawn in her eyes.

She yawns and covers her mouth, then motions for me to come inside. "Yeah, come on in. Are you thirsty?"

As she walks a few feet into the house, she turns to see if I'm following. I'm not. Something doesn't feel right about this. What single woman invites a strange man into her home?

"In or out, buddy? You'll let in the bugs if you just stand there with the door open, and air conditioning isn't exactly free." She yawns again and swipes her hands over her eyes. "Coffee or tea?"

I clear my throat and step inside, closing the door behind me—after I remind myself that I have a gun. If she has anything planned, I'll handle her.

"Neither," I say. "I'm not really big on caffeine. I'll just take some tap water, if it's not too much trouble."

She shrugs. "Suit yourself, but if you're worried about what caffeine will do to your body, I doubt you want what's in tap water. Take a seat at the kitchen table."

"I don't really care about the caffeine, but I stopped drinking the stuff when my wife got pregnant. She said it wasn't good for the baby, so I figured I could support her." I sit down as instructed, not sure why I'm sharing such private information with the woman. I guess some subconscious part of myself wants to ensure I'm humanized in her eyes. Or maybe I just really miss my wife.

"You're married?" she asks.

I nod. "My wife passed, but I'm still married."

The woman freezes, then continues shuffling around in the kitchen. As she prepares the drinks, I look around at the odd decor. A ceramic rooster crows at me from the table's center. On the counter, right beside the toaster, stands a large goose cookie jar. The finishing touch is a pig painting that details the different cuts of pork.

"Farmhouse chic?" I say as I study the odds and ends. "Way out in the woods like this, you could have the actual farm."

She sits beside me at the table and slides the mug into my hands. Despite asking for water, I look down into a well of dark coffee. I haven't had the stuff since before my wife's death, so it feels wrong to drink it now, but the woman is staring. I raise the mug and take a sip.

"It's decaf." She plucks up her mug. "Sometimes I want a warm cup at night, but I don't want to struggle sleeping." She laughs and shakes her head. "I always have trouble sleeping anyway, so it doesn't really help, but I tell myself it does."

I chuckle to myself and take another pull from the warm mug.

"Is that why you did it?" she asks after a quiet moment. "Your wife, I mean. Was her death the catalyst for the murder?"

Lowering the mug, I clear my throat. "Excuse me?"

"That's the question I'm dying to answer here. Why did you kill that bank CEO?"

"I think you may have the wrong man."

She shakes her head and says, "No, you're the right one. I should know. I drew your face."

As if this is a completely normal thing to say, she rises from the table and returns with a sketch. And she's right. That's definitely me.

I raise the mug and chug the rest of the coffee. She's probably already called the fucking cops, and I'm well and truly screwed. I never should have stopped here. I should have kept—

"I made this too," she says as she shoves a purple piece of paper into my hands. She sounds so proud, but I'm terrified as I look down and see my images plastered all over it. "I guess I don't really need those anymore, though. Not now that the real thing is right in front of me."

A wave of dizziness washes over me. This wasn't how this was supposed to go. I was just going to come in, have a drink, maybe a bite of food, and pretend to make a phone call while I cased the place for something to sell for some gas money to get me out of the state.

"Are you going to turn me in?" I ask.

She smiles at me and grabs the papers. "I'm not sure. I haven't decided yet. How are you feeling?"

I shake my head to will the dizzy feeling away, but it's only growing. I pull the mug closer and look inside. Tiny white granules cling to the bottom of the glass, and judging by the bitter bite to the coffee, I don't think it's sugar.

"You drugged me?" I teeter on the edge of the chair as I try to stand. My hand goes for the gun in my waistband, but my hands are lead. My feet are lead. Everything is fucking lead, and nothing works.

"Whoops! You won't be needing that," she says as she snatches the gun away from me. "You might want to sit down. That shit hits really fast and pretty hard, and I don't have what I need to patch you up if you split something open. I mean, I work at a hospital, but I'm no nurse."

Her voice fades as I crumple to the floor. I've gone from the frying pan to the fire, and now I've transitioned to . . . whatever this is. Maybe turning myself in isn't such a bad idea. I have no idea what this woman has in store, and I don't think I want to find out.

Chapter Four

Grey

Something clicks in the distance, and bright light flashes through my eyelids. After a brief whirring sound, the room goes quiet again. Seconds later, the sounds repeat. I force my eyes open. I'm on a bed, and standing at the foot, with a Polaroid camera dangling around her neck and two newly minted pictures in her hands, stands the woman who drugged me.

"Gosh, you're very photogenic," she says as she studies the pictures. "Have you ever done any modeling? Your facial structure is really nice."

I try to sit up, but something around my neck holds me to the bed. I reach toward my throat and realize I'm wearing a metal collar.

"Oh, goodness, let me lengthen that chain," she says, as if that's the most natural thing to say to someone you've taken hostage. She gets on her stomach and slithers under the bed. Metal clanks and clangs, and a few seconds later, she emerges once more. "There. You can move around now." She smiles at me, looking very pleased with herself.

I move to sit up, and she's right. I have more room now. Not enough to escape this bedroom, of course, but at least I'm not forced into a prone position.

After blinking to clear the medication's haze, I look around. A single window lets some sunlight into the room. Judging by the fading light, I've been out for several hours. I lie on a white wrought-iron bed with a mattress that seems to sway with my movements, but at least it's comfortable. A white dresser stands against one wall, and a large vanity dominates the wall in front of the bed.

"How long do you plan to keep me chained to your bed?" I ask. It's a fair question.

She places the pictures on top of the dresser and raises the camera again. "I haven't decided." The bulb flashes, and the machine whirs as it spits out another picture. "Shit, I'm out of film."

"How many pictures have you taken?"

Instead of answering my question, she places the photo with the others and leaves the room. She returns seconds later with something black in her hands. The camera still dangles from her neck.

"Do me a favor," she says as she tosses the black object into my lap. "Put this on."

Raising the clump of black fabric, I realize it's my mask. She must have gone through my coat pockets. My eyes narrow on her, but I oblige and slide the mask over my face.

"Now smile," she says.

So I do.

She shakes her head and groans. "No, no. Not like that. Wider. Happier."

I do my best impression of a happier Grey, which isn't easy, given my current circumstances.

"There it is," she moans. "That smile. Fuck, it's perfect." She snaps another picture, then sits on the side of the bed.

"Can I stop smiling now?" I ask. "I'd really just like to know what's happening here." I finger the collar around my neck. "And maybe why you have some serious hostage devices."

She starts to giggle, then covers her mouth. "Oh, I'm not in the business of kidnapping people. My ex had a captivity fetish, and when he broke my heart and left me for someone else, I didn't have the heart to throw everything away. I just never thought it would come in handy like this."

"Like what?"

She holds her hands toward me. "You, here, in my house. You're my meal ticket, Grey."

"How do you—"

"Know your name?" She smirks. "You're all over the news now. They know your name, what car you drive. What they haven't said is why you killed that bank lady. That's what I want to find out."

"Before you turn me in."

"If your reward amount rises, definitely. Right now, you're small beans. Crime Stoppers has offered a whopping five grand for your head, but I have a feeling that will triple by tomorrow morning."

I pull off my mask and sigh.

"Put these on," she says as she drops some leg shackles onto the bed. "I want to show you something."

What a strange woman I've forced my presence upon. She looks positively rabid. Attractive as fuck, but rabid.

"Come on," she says, and something about the fire in her green eyes makes me extremely uncomfortable.

Raising the leg shackles, I study their design and look for any flaws. If I can find a way to escape this psychotic lady, I will. Then I'll steal her car and never stop at a stranger's house again. I've learned my lesson.

My wife was never into anything kinky, and neither was I, but I don't think these leg shackles came from a sex shop. They're heavy as fuck, and thick to boot. When I strap these around my ankles, I'm not getting out of them.

"Do you need some help?" she asks. "They aren't that complicated, you know. They're just handcuffs for your feet."

With a sigh, I clamp the first cuff and close my eyes as the locking mechanism catches. I try to leave it a little loose, but she's too smart for that. Once I've secured both ankles, she checks them and tightens them a few clicks.

"Nice try, Grey. Now lean back so I can unlock your collar."

I do as I'm told, and she frees my neck. Cool air rushes to greet the sweaty ring around my throat, and my skin welcomes the sensation.

I follow her into the living room. My mouth drops open as I see her coffee table. It's covered in . . . me. More printouts of me and screen grabs from the TV. And instant photos. So many instant photos.

She's unhinged.

"Take a seat," she says as she motions to the couch.

I sit on the faded blue couch that I glimpsed through the window a few feet away. That feels like it happened to someone else a lifetime ago. The woman sits beside me, and I realize I don't know her name. I'm not sure why I even want to know her name, considering the predicament she's placed me in, but I do. So I ask.

"Briar," she says. "My mom had a fascination with

Sleeping Beauty. How ironic that she would birth a child who can't sleep for shit." She chuckles to herself as she grabs the television remote and sits beside me as if we're old friends. "What's your origin story? Do you have a brother named Greige or a sister named Chartreuse?"

I shrug. "No idea. I was adopted. My name was the only thing my mother gave me, so my adoptive parents let me keep it."

She shuffles to face me, the television forgotten. "Oh, did you have a horrible upbringing? Were your adoptive parents abusive? Is that why you were driven to kill?"

"What? No. You watch too much Lifetime." I sigh and fold my hands in my lap. "My adoptive parents were wonderful. I had an excellent upbringing, and I felt very loved. Why I killed the lady isn't important to anyone but me, and I don't care what other people think of what I've done. My reasons were my reasons."

The excitement evaporates from her face, and she curls her lip. "Maybe you're only worth five grand after all."

If she's trying to bait me into explaining why I killed the bitch, she'll be dangling that hook for a while. Nobody cared about my sob story when the bank came to take everything from us, so no one deserves to hear it now. It's my private tale, a story etched into my fucking soul. It's mine. No one else's.

Briar settles back in her seat and raises the remote, but before she can turn on the television, someone knocks at the door. Our eyes widen, and we both look at each other.

"Are you expecting someone?" I whisper.

She shakes her head.

The knock comes again, followed by a booming voice. "New York State Police! Is anyone home?"

Chapter Five

Briar

I hurry to stand, then motion for Grey to do the same. If he shouts and alerts the officers, this could all be over right now. And I don't want that. The moment I find out why he committed the murder, I'm turning him in and enjoying that sweet, sweet reward money, but until that moment, he's mine.

"Just a minute!" I yell toward the door. "I'm not dressed for company!"

I grab Grey's hand and yank him toward the basement door. When he realizes we aren't headed back to the bedroom, he digs his heels into the floor and refuses to take another step. He shakes his head, though I'm thankful he doesn't voice his protests.

"It's soundproof down there, and I don't trust you to keep quiet in the bedroom," I whisper. "It's either the basement or I'll tell him you held a gun on me."

His shoulders droop, and he grits his teeth as he makes a strangling motion toward my throat, but he starts walking

Thankfully, he doesn't think about the fact that the cop might find it a bit odd that I've shackled his ankles. I flick on the light and open the second door at the bottom of the stairs. Grey's eyes widen as he steps into the room.

"What? I told you already. My ex was into some kinky shit." I lead him to the back wall and motion for him to step closer so that I can swap his leg shackles for a leg spreader. He won't be able to waddle more than a few feet once I lock him into that.

"No, I draw the line at that thing," he says as he points at the spreader. "I've watched enough porn to know what that is."

"Fine. Just stay put and be quiet," I tell him before heading up the stairs and closing—and locking—the doors leading into the basement.

My fingers shake as I grip the doorknob to the front door. Fuck, everything shakes. Men in uniform stand outside, and I have a murderer with leg shackles in my basement. Nervous is an understatement. But I open the door and force my best smile onto my face.

"Ah, good evening, officers."

"Hello, ma'am," one of the men says as he leans in and looks past me. Shadows cover everything, including my art projects scattered all over the coffee table. My home is dark except for the hall light leading toward my bedroom. It looks as if I came from one place and one place only. Which is good.

"How can I help you?" I ask, interrupting his in-depth scan of my home.

"We're looking for the man who shot the bank CEO yesterday. He's been on the run, and one of our units thought they saw his car come down your driveway earlier today."

"And you didn't keep following him?" I place my hand on my chest, gripping my invisible pearls. "I've been napping most of the day because I haven't felt well. I called out of work because I'm sick. Maybe you two should give my house a thorough walkthrough to be sure he didn't sneak in. I could have died!"

The officers glance at each other, both of them seemingly alarmed by my sudden histrionics. The shorter of the two takes a step backward. "His car isn't here, ma'am, and we have other houses to check. If he'd broken in, I'm sure you'd have heard him. He's a senseless killer, so you probably wouldn't be alive to talk to us. More than likely, he drove down your driveway, then turned around and kept moving."

I take a step into the cool night air and wiggle my toes on the wooden porch. I look left and then right, then left again. "Well . . . if you're sure."

The taller officer reaches into his pocket and hands me his card. "We're sure. If you see anything, though, please give us a call."

"Are you positive you don't need to look around?" I peer toward the garage, where I swapped my car for Grey's several hours ago. "I could bake some cookies for your time."

The shorter officer clears his throat and turns away, clearly put off by my desperate-woman routine. "You'll be fine. Have a nice evening, ma'am."

I nod, step inside, and close the door. When their headlights brighten my living room, then turn toward my bedroom, I step toward the window and peek through a gap in the curtain until their taillights disappear. Once I'm certain they're gone and won't be back, I hurry for the basement.

"How'd it go?" he asks as I shut the door behind me.

"They just wanted to know if I'd seen you."

His eyes widen. "Oh, fuck. My car. How'd you handle that?"

"I drove it into the garage hours ago. Don't worry so much."

"I'll keep worrying, thanks. Being too complacent is what got me into this fucking mess in the first place."

My ears perk up. "Is that why you killed her? Did you default on your payments or something? Did you—"

"It's none of your concern. Could you stop fucking asking already? I don't want to talk about it, especially with someone who plans to turn me in." He flops onto his ass and looks around. "Are you gonna feed me or anything? I'm fucking starving."

"If you want something from me, you'll need to give me something in return."

I go to smirk, but the smile slides off my face as he gets to his feet and steps into me until my back is against the wall. When I can't walk backward anymore, he keeps coming, sandwiching me between body heat and concrete.

"I want to make something very clear, Briar. The arrangement you believe you have is not the arrangement you have in actuality. My legs may be shackled, but my hands are very much not. If I want to strangle the life from your lungs and snatch that key from your pocket, I will." He leans closer, until his breath is close enough to send goosebumps over my skin. "You have a tame tiger in the basement. Tame, but not domesticated. You'd do well to remember that."

His mention of the shackles around his legs brings the smirk back to my face. I reach into my pocket, grip a small remote, and depress the largest button. Grey screams as his legs buckle beneath him, sending him to the floor.

"What the—"

I press the button again when he tries to stand, and he lets out another scream before sitting back on his elbows and panting up at me. As I squat beside him, I smile.

"A tiger, huh?" I flick a quiff of dark hair from his forehead. "You're looking more like a house cat to me."

He sighs and looks away from me. That's fine. I've delivered my message, and he heard it. The next time he wants to intimidate me, he'll think twice. The leg shackles aren't the only device rigged with a pretty hardcore electric shock.

I step toward a toolbox and pull a set of wrist cuffs from the second drawer. They're just cuffs, with no chain holding them together, but they pack a little secret.

"Give me your wrists," I demand when I reach Grey's side again.

He rolls his eyes and holds out his hands. "What is this, some sort of tracking device?"

"No." I strap the first cuff over his wrist, then secure it with a latch. These don't lock, unfortunately, but they don't really need to. Not as long as I'm supervising. "They provide another point of control."

"How the fuck was this even useful in the bedroom?"

I shrug. "I dunno. I never got to try them. I found out he cheated, and then we broke up before we could use them. Maybe it's for pleasure delay."

"Pleasure delay?"

"Yeah, like edging. If you started beating your dick, I'd shock you each time you got close to coming."

"Wanna try it?" he says, and his hands go toward his pants.

With bated breath, I wait for him to reveal his cock. I'm curious, what can I say? Fucking shoot me.

But then his jaw drops, and he looks up at me. "You were going to let me pull it out!"

"What? No I wasn't!" I hurry to my feet and start for the door.

He laughs behind me, and I hate what that sound does to my insides. "Don't try to hide it now. You wanted to see my d—"

The crackle of electricity silences him, and he grits his teeth as he loses control of his arms.

"I'll be down in a bit with some dinner. I hope you like ramen."

With that, I shut off the light and hurry out of the basement before the urge to turn him in overtakes me. That reward amount still isn't high enough yet. And I still don't have the answers I need.

Chapter Six

Grey

Once I've finished the ramen, I push the bowl away from me on the concrete floor and lean against the wall. When you finally eat after days of going without, it does a number on your insides. My stomach clamps down in another cramp, and I try not to make a sound as I ride it out.

"Something bothering you?" she asks as she places my bowl beneath hers. "You don't look so hot."

I pull my legs up and wrap my arms around my knees. "Considering I haven't used the bathroom since I got here, my bladder pains are pretty understandable."

"Oh!" She hurries to stand, then leaves the room. A few minutes later, she returns with something blue in her hands. My stomach sinks as I realize what it is.

I shake my head. "I'm not pissing in a bucket."

"Then I guess you'll just piss in your pants. You aren't going back upstairs. Not now that I know the police saw your car turn in here." She drops the bucket and pushes it toward me.

"I told you. I'm not going to piss in a bucket. You have my gun. I'm not stupid. Take me to the bathroom."

"No, *I* am not stupid. That's why I refuse to take you upstairs. If you really wanted to overpower me and take the gun, there's enough shit up there to help you accomplish that."

"And where would I run? Do you think I want to be out there, dealing with cops at every turn? I'm safer here."

It's a lie. Kind of. I mean, this is still better than prison, I guess.

She disappears again and shows up with my gun in her hand. She aims it at me. "Upstairs," she says, motioning up the basement steps.

I scramble to my feet and walk ahead of her. As I pass her, I glance at the gun. The safety is off, so she clearly knows what she's doing. And she means business.

We reach the ground floor of her home, and she gestures to the left. I follow her directions to the bathroom, and I'm grateful when she lets me go in by myself, though she stays just outside the door. When I go to close it, she shakes her head.

"Leave the door open."

I sigh and turn to unzip my jeans, pull out my dick, and piss. I hope she enjoys the view, since she can't stop staring at me.

"Do you think you can keep me here forever?" I put my hand against the wall and lean into it.

"I don't think I can keep you forever, but I'd like to keep you as long as I can. At least until your reward rises to a respectable level and I learn why you killed the woman."

"Do they have any leads?"

"No. A lot of social media experts weigh in, though. Most people view you as a hero."

I cock my head. "What do you mean? I killed someone."

"You didn't kill *someone*. You killed the epitome of a power imbalance. The head of abuse of federal institutions, like banks."

I scoff. "She's still a person. Well, was."

"People think of you as a hero without a cape. They believe you were sticking it to the man at a time when the man really needed to get stuck."

"Is that what you think of me?"

She offers a noncommittal shrug, and I pull my gaze from her. I'm no hero. I'm the villain.

"You're a little bit of a psycho. You know that, right?" I shake off my dick and tuck it inside my pants.

"Yeah, I do."

I'm being kind. Someone who holds a murderer hostage while his reward money rises is so far removed from psychosis. She's in her own field of crazy.

Taking a moment, I glance around the bathroom, looking for anything that could help me escape this precarious situation. With her staring at me like this, that's pretty hard to do.

"Can I take a shower?" I ask, hoping that will afford me some privacy. "I haven't done more than wipe up in a gas station bathroom for ages."

"Sure, go ahead."

I clear my throat and hold out my hands. "Any chance I could get a little privacy?"

The gun's barrel rides down my body as she considers my request. She glances at the small window in the shower, then realizes I can't squeeze through it. "Sure, but don't do anything stupid."

"More stupid than killing an elite?"

She smiles before removing my shackles and wrist cuffs, then leaves the bathroom. As soon as she closes the door, I look for a way to escape. Her beauty is only rivaled by her fucked-up mind, and I'd be lying if I said she doesn't intimidate me. I'm probably safer outside with the cops, now that I think about it.

Despite knowing I won't fit, I study the window anyway. Even if I had narrow shoulders, I'd have to break bones to fit through that gap. Not a bad option, considering the alternatives. Then again . . . maybe her fascination could play in my favor. Maybe I've been coming at this from the wrong angle.

She's a single woman, clearly still upset by the breakup with her ex. I mean, why else would she keep the sex dungeon intact? If she's lonely, I could use that to my advantage. I can get close to her, drop her guard, and make my escape.

I look in the mirror and frown. If I want to seduce her, I'll need to clean myself up a bit. The rugged look is fine, but the homeless look? Not so much. I grab a razor and fruity-smelling gel foam and begin by lining up my stubble. When I come out of this bathroom, Briar won't know what hit her.

Chapter Seven

Briar

W hen he finally steps out of the bathroom, he looks like a new man. Literally. I found him attractive before, but now that he's cleaned up, I'll need to make sure he doesn't catch me staring. He's male perfection.

I offer him some clothes that were still hanging around from my ex. Surprisingly, they fit. Even the jeans hug his hips just right. The shirt's a little small, though. My ex didn't have defined muscles.

Or tattoos.

I study the word running down his left bicep. It says Delinquent, but I don't know if that refers to his actions or a missed payment. Has he always been a criminal, or was this latest performance the act of a desperate man, as I believe?

His right bicep has a word etched into it as well, but I can't read it. It's covered by his dirty clothes, which he holds toward me.

"What does that one say?" I nod toward his arm as I accept his clothes.

He looks down and twists his wrist, turning his entire arm so that I can see the word fully. Foreclosure.

"So that's it," I say. "The bank took your house, and that's why you killed her."

He nods and sighs. "Yes, that's part of it."

A little thrill runs through me. I've unearthed a piece of the skeleton in his closet, but I won't be content until I've dragged the entire thing into the light. If little acts of kindness, like a shower, will net me better results, I'll have to be nicer, I guess.

Nicer, but not stupid.

"Let's get you back into your cuffs," I say. I drop the leg shackles at his feet, along with the wrist cuffs, and then I aim the gun at his handsome face.

He obliges without argument, stepping into and latching the leg shackles. Once he's secured in the basement, I gather his clothes once more and start upstairs. I lock both doors behind me on my way up. Instead of heading to the laundry room, however, I return to the bathroom.

Water still beads on the glass from his shower. I try not to think about the fact that some of this water has touched his bare skin as I drop his clothes to the floor, then strip out of mine and step inside. I breathe in the scent. Yes, the smell is the same as the soaps I use on a daily basis, but it's also different. A masculine, earthy undertone lingers in the air.

My head tips forward and touches the wall. The beads of water latch onto my skin, then travel toward my lips. I open my mouth and let them land on my tongue. Just feeling this close to his naked body drives me to the most indecent thoughts.

I want him. More than just his secrets and his

dangerous presence. More than the money his soul can bring. I want him in ways I shouldn't.

I step into the wall and let my bare nipples graze the warm ceramic as I turn the handle. Cold water rushes out of the faucet, and I imagine him inside this space with me. His hands on every inch of my body. The water heats in time with my thoughts, and I turn on the shower.

God, I wish I could shower with him, but that would be stupid. Trying anything sexual would be a major misstep. For multiple reasons, I can't lose him. Besides, he thinks I'm crazy. And as I back away from the wall after tasting him via droplets of water left behind in my shower, I can't deny that he's kind of right.

I suppose this could be misplaced daddy issues. My father fought against Big Bank too, and he saved our family. My father did something horrible, and my mother and I viewed him as a hero for it. That isn't so different from how people online view Grey.

After I've scrubbed every ounce of desire from my pores, I gather our dirty clothes and carry them to the laundry room. As I'm dumping everything into the washer, I hesitate when the soft boxer briefs appear in my hands. I grind the fabric between my finger and thumb. I imagine being the damn things.

Against my will, I find myself bringing the boxers up to my nose. I inhale deeply and suffocate in his scent, which is used and dirty and musty. But not in a bad way. Instead of turning on the wash, I find myself losing my grip on sanity as I step into his used boxers.

I close the lid, climb up, and lean back on the washer. I touch myself over the fabric, rubbing the filthy material between my pussy lips, grinding down on my excited clit.

Electricity courses through the thin material and buzzes against me.

"Grey," I whisper as I get closer to an edge I shouldn't be on. This is ethically wrong.

Even so, I come to thoughts of his body moving against mine as an earth-shattering orgasm rattles the metal beneath me.

I climb off the washer, step out of the boxers, and look at them. Streaks of my come paint them, and for some reason, I can't throw them in the wash. I want them against me forever. But I do throw them in, along with his shirt.

My guilt washes away with his as our clothes intermingle, but my newfound longing for him flows deeper than can be cleansed. This is going to be a problem.

Chapter Eight

Grey

Lightning strikes just outside the basement window that's too small for me to squeeze through. Believe me. I tried. Thunder claps, and I jump from my skin at the sheer ferocity of the sound. The house seems to groan above me, mirroring my unease. The next flash of light is accompanied by a loud boom, followed by total darkness.

The power has gone out.

A door opens with a high-pitched whine, and footsteps creak on the stairs. Moments later, the second door swishes open and closes again, followed by the locks engaging. A flashlight kicks on, and the beam bounces around the room until it lands on me. I shuffle the chain connecting my legs to the wall to show her I'm still confined. Satisfied, she moves toward the breaker box and begins flipping switches, but nothing happens.

As she continues fiddling with the fuse box, I squat and gather the long chain in my hands, then turn my attention back to her. The flashlight's beam offers just enough light that I can see how cute she looks in her dark leggings and an oversized sleep shirt that exposes her right shoulder.

Stop that. She's not cute. She abducted you.

But must those things be mutually exclusive? Can't she be both dangerous and adorable? And it's not as if I'm one to talk. I committed a murder less than forty-eight hours ago, and I've yet to feel any genuine remorse for what I've done.

"The power's out," she finally says. "Maybe it's best if you come upstairs for the night. I'm not going to get any sleep now, so you can take the bed. It'll be better than that pile of blankets." She motions to the folded fabric lying on the concrete floor.

Gripping the flashlight, she steps closer and pulls the gun from the back of her waistband, then aims it at me. She sets the flashlight on the ground, keeping the gun's muzzle aimed at my abdomen as she goes to unlock the chain attaching me to the wall. Unfortunately, she can't do this with only one hand. She sets the gun by her foot, and I listen for the sound of freedom as the lock disengages.

Before she can straighten herself to face me, I leap for her. The key clangs to the floor. I snatch the chain from her hand and wrap it around her neck, pulling her tight against my body. She doesn't fight within my grasp, even as the pressure tightens around her throat.

"You won't do this," she pants. "You only hurt people who hurt you."

"What makes you think that?"

She sucks in a breath. "It's just a feeling, Grey. I can't explain it. You won't hurt me, and we both know it."

I tighten my hold on the chain. "And what do you call chaining me to a wall, hmm? You're holding me hostage."

"I'm not . . . hurting you," she grits out. "I'm keeping you safe."

"Yeah, until the bidding gets high enough for your liking. Then you'll trade me off for a wad of cash." I release my hold on the chain, push her away from me, and go for the gun. "I don't need you to protect me, little psycho."

She stumbles forward a few steps, then turns to face me as she finds her footing. "You don't understand. If I don't do this, I'll . . ."

"You'll what?" I squat and grab the flashlight, then stand and shine it into her face. Are those tears?

"Just fucking shoot me," she says. "I can't lose this fucking house. I'm as good as dead if I do."

I can't deny the absolute defeat in her eyes. It's an emotion I recognize because I've been in her shoes. I've done despicable things because of walking in those same footsteps.

"They're threatening foreclosure?" I ask.

Her legs give out, and she collapses to the floor. "What do you care? We can't both win here. I need the money, and you need your freedom. To be honest, I don't think I could have turned you in, anyway."

"Maybe we can figure something out. Maybe there's some mutually beneficial solution we haven't thought of."

She shrugs. "My life is fucking over. It doesn't matter, and this was a stupid idea on my part." Her head thumps against the wall as she leans back. "Could you just give me one small thing?"

"What's that?"

The silence stretches out, and then she takes a deep breath. "Tell me why you did it."

"There's nothing to tell."

"Bullshit." Her head pulls forward again, and she's

looking right at me. "You could have killed me just now, and you didn't. You would have been justified, too. That tells me you had a very good reason for killing that bitch, and I want to know what it was."

"What do you expect from me? The reasons don't matter. Killing her didn't fix anything. When people say that murder doesn't solve problems, they aren't lying. It solved nothing, and I feel worse for it." I bite my inner lip. Maybe it won't hurt to give her a tiny piece of the puzzle. "Remember those NINJA loans?"

"No income, no job, no assets," we say in unison.

"It ruined my life," I continue. "And not just my life . . ." My voice fades out as my heart begins to ache.

"Those loans ruined a lot of people's lives," Briar says. "When I was little, the bank tried to foreclose on our home."

"How'd you guys manage?"

A sly grin slides onto her face, made almost eerie by the flashlight's glow. "My dad robbed a bank to save the house."

My jaw falls open, and I can't believe what I'm hearing. "No fucking way. Did he get caught?"

She shakes her head, sending her red hair around her face. "He was never discovered, but he and my mother died in a car crash a couple of years later, so it didn't matter anyway. They still lost the house, and I was placed in foster care." She looks around the basement, then offers me a sad smile. "I got the house back, though."

The pieces of the puzzle are fitting together now. Her desperation is understandable because it was once my desperation. It's a desperation too many Americans have become familiar with. We are sold the American dream at a price they know we can't afford.

I slide the gun across the floor to her. It bumps against her shoe, and she looks at it.

"What are you doing?" she asks, and I can't answer her. Because I have no fucking clue.

I had the upper hand, and now I'm giving it back to her if for no other reason than I'm not the monster I need to be. She's right. I'm not some hardened killer who takes a life for the sake of it.

"I really don't want to go to fucking prison," I say into the darkness. "If we can find some way to avoid that where you can still keep the house . . ."

And that's when it hits me.

I still have access to the cams in Gloria's house. Maybe the solution to her problem lies there. And if she has a solution, maybe I do too.

"Do you have a computer you'd let me use?" I ask. "I'd like to show you something."

She motions toward the ceiling. "Yeah, but there's no power. The Wi-Fi won't work."

"Your phone?"

Her hand goes into her pocket, and she pulls it out. "Dead. I kind of forgot to charge it when I was busy kidnapping a murderer. My bad."

I let out a soft laugh. I can't help it. She might be out of her fucking gourd, but she's also likeable as hell.

"Well, I guess we can go upstairs now," she says. "But if you think I'm letting you go, you're sadly mistaken. I like you, Grey, but I like . . ." She hesitates, then says, "I like this house and the memories it holds a little more." She plucks up the gun and stuffs it into her pants. At least she isn't holding it on me anymore.

I nod and follow her upstairs, but I get the sneaking suspicion that she's holding something back. Maybe I'm not the only person with secrets I'm not ready to share.

Chapter Nine

Briar

I nviting him into my bed was probably a terrible idea, but I'm tired and I need to keep an eye on him. I put him back in his metal collar, then climbed beside him in bed. Part of me worried he would tell me to sleep on the couch, but he didn't. He just turned onto his side and faced away from me.

Not that I'll sleep. Being tired and being sleepy have two very different meanings in my world, and I'm the former, not the latter.

Lightning fills the room, and the loud crack of thunder follows closely after. Storms don't frighten me the way they used to scare my mother, but the unexpected sound still makes me jump. And maybe I'm just a *little* scared.

Grey turns to face me. "You okay?"

"I'm fine." I pull the blanket tighter around me.

"You don't seem fine. I was almost asleep, but you keep getting jumpy every time it thunders."

"No I don't."

His arm shoots out and goes over my midsection. I try to pull away as he tugs me closer to him.

"Stop fighting me, Briar. Just relax."

So I do. I stop fighting and allow him to pull me against him. His breath falls on my neck, hot and heavy.

"Can you feel my heart beating against your back?"

I close my eyes and focus on the point where our skin connects, which makes me aware of the fact that he's not wearing a shirt and I've traded my bulky sleep shirt for a thin cami. Our skin connects in other places as well. Places that make me a little too warm.

But then . . . I feel it. A gentle *thump, thump, thump* flutters against my spine, like a bird flapping its wings. His hand presses against my chest, and I realize he's doing the same thing. He's feeling my beating heart.

"Breathe with me, now," he whispers. "Feel my breath and match it."

His chest expands against my back, and I breathe in. When his chest recedes, I exhale.

"Just like that." His gravelly whisper reaches through the darkness and caresses me.

As his palm splays over my chest, his fingertips brush against my left nipple. It wasn't intentional, but that touch sends a shiver up my spine. Goosebumps rise on my skin, and my nipples harden to tight points. I'm sure he feels them because parts of him harden behind me.

I pretend to readjust. In reality, I want to push my ass against his girth and be sure I feel what I think I feel. Something thick and hard presses against me, and a moan sneaks out of my throat.

Embarrassment warms my cheeks, but that feeling fades when he presses on my shoulder until I'm on my back. He hovers above me, as much as the metal collar and its chain will allow, then lowers his face until his lips brush mine in a chaste kiss.

When the lightning flashes and thunder rumbles, I don't jump. I'm too scared this moment will end if I do more than lie here and wait to see what he does next. We stand at a precipice. He's about to jump or back away, and I don't want to influence either reaction. If he wants me, I want him to take me.

But then I have my answer when his hand snakes up my shirt and finds my breast. He squeezes the flesh in his hand and deepens the kiss. My fingers hurry toward the nape of his neck, then dive into his dark hair as I pull him closer.

That's when he pulls away.

"Briar, I'm sorry," he says as he flops onto his back and presses the backs of his hands into his eyes. "I don't know what I was thinking. You're vulnerable right now, and I shouldn't take advantage of that. I'm vulnerable right now too. We can't do this."

The fuck we can't! I climb over him and straddle his waist. "I don't know about *can't*. You seem pretty capable." I reach back and squeeze his stiff cock.

His hands rise to my waist, and he presses me down on his lap. "Fuck, don't make this harder than it has to be. I really shouldn't do this."

"Sometimes the worst possible thing we could do is the best thing we could do." I grind my hips and moan as the friction travels up my spine. "What if you fuck me so good that I can't bear the thought of turning you in? This could benefit both of us."

"You plan to keep me around as your personal sex toy?" His eyebrow rises, and I nearly get off right here.

"Only if you make me come."

"Is that a promise?"

I bite my lip. I don't break promises, and I ensure that by rarely making them. Would an orgasm really be worth losing my house and my life?

When I look into Grey's eyes, the answer is yes.

"If you make me come, I promise to *consider* alternatives to turning you in. Does that work?"

He takes a deep breath, closes his eyes, and considers my proposal. When his eyes open again, a flash of lightning plays across his bare chest as he nods his head. "That works."

I slide off his lap and lie on my back again. He turns onto his side and looks down at me.

"What are you doing?" he asks. "I thought you wanted to fuck me?"

"No, the deal was that you would make me come. Chop, chop!" I spread my legs. "You have a lot of work ahead of you."

He scoffs. "Bring that pussy over here where my mouth is. I'll have your thighs quivering in no time."

I smirk and clamber over him so I can straddle his chest. I use the chain as leverage as I climb up his body until my knees fall on either side of his head. I don't take off my shorts, though. I don't want him to see the scars my ex left on my ass. Instead, I pull the crotch of my shorts aside, and he gets right to work on my slit. His warm tongue spreads my lips and finds my clit as his hands hook around my thighs.

"Sit on my face, little psycho," he growls, and the vibration rumbles against me.

I spasm with each syllable, wrapping the chain around my hand and tugging. It lifts the collar around his neck and only once he takes a few heavy breaths do I realize I'm choking him.

Well, this is a fun little surprise.

I squeeze off his air, and despite the lack of oxygen, he continues devouring me. "You want air, Grey? You want to breathe?"

He nods, moving everything against me as he does.

"Then make me come."

I don't *actually* want to kill the guy, so I release the tension on the chain and let him gasp a few times before I tighten it again. He's really putting a lot of trust in his kidnapper. Either way, I ride his breathless mouth and tongue until my thighs quiver, just as he assured me they would. I release the chain, and his warm breath bathes my clit. When I pull the chain once more, I focus on the warm wetness of his mouth as he eats me.

He slaps my thigh, and I release the chain.

"What?"

"You aren't sitting hard enough. I don't want to breathe when you release that chain. Fucking sit on my face."

If he wants to die buried in my pussy, who am I to deny his dying wish?

So I do it. I press all of my weight onto his face and grip the chain again. Now I'm certain he can't even gasp without a mouthful of my flesh.

I put my other hand on the headboard and ride his mouth and tongue until I see stars behind my eyelids. Inhuman screams leave my body as he makes me come on his face. Even as he smacks my thigh to let me know he's suffocating, I can't stop this orgasm he started. My knuckles whiten as I squeeze the headboard, and the chain wrapped around my hand begins to pinch my flesh. My entire body tenses before relaxing in the most surreal way I've never felt.

Then I realize he's digging his nails into my thighs.

"Oh, sorry!" I say as I unwrap the chain and lean back so he can breathe.

"There's worse . . . ways to go . . . I guess," he says through gasps of air.

I climb down his body and put my hand on his cock. He's hard, but the moment I try to pull his sweatpants down, his dick deflates in front of me. Well, that does nothing for my self-esteem.

"Briar," he whispers. "It's not you."

It sure the fuck isn't, and I think I know what might help him. "I have an idea."

I pull myself off his lap and run to grab a candle. After placing it on the bedside table, I light it and smile as the room is bathed in a yellow glow. I reach between the bed and the table and feel for what he needs. My fingers grip the soft material, and I pull it into the light.

"What's that?" he asks.

"Your mask."

"Do I even want to know why my mask is beside your bed?"

Not one to hide my sexual secrets, I tell him. "I've been masturbating with it."

He just stares at me, then says, "So how will it help me?"

"This mask gave you the confidence you needed to commit that murder, so it stands to reason that it could help you now, in much the same way. For whatever reason, you think that fucking me is wrong, just like you knew killing that woman was wrong. I want you to put on the mask and repeat history. Make my body a fucking crime scene, Grey."

I half-expect him to recoil. He hasn't loved mentions of his crime so far. But he doesn't. He just lifts his hand, snatches the mask away, and puts it over his head.

God, he's handsome without his mask, but with it? He's irresistible. There's something almost menacing about the way his eyes are the only visible piece of his face. With this mask on, he's a murderer instead of a man who committed a desperate homicide.

Arousal drips down my thighs.

I straddle his body and grind my pussy over the front of his pants. His hands glide down my sides as he lengthens and hardens beneath me. When I tug down the front of his sweatpants, he remains hard this time. I run my hand along the soft, silky skin and wrap my fingers around him.

"You know what I want you to do with that," he says. "It's the same thing I wanted you to do to my face."

"And what's that?" I bite my lip.

"Sit on my fucking cock."

I like this side of him. I like the confidence that mask gives him. So I push the crotch of my shorts aside again, rub his cock through my wet slit, and press him against my entrance. A moan leaves my mouth as I sit on him fully, and the groan that leaves him makes me pulse around him.

Fuck, I like that sound. It sounds like he's been waiting for this. And wanting it too.

He fills me entirely as I ride him, up and down, forward and backward, until I'm dripping down his length. His hands squeeze my hips as I buck on top of him, and then he grips my hair and pulls me against him. My hard nipples press against my cami, yearning to touch his skin.

"Pull my mask up a bit, little psycho," he grits out.

I reach up and raise the bottom of his mask. His full lips pop out from beneath the fabric, and he drags me into him by my hair, bringing my mouth to his.

I pull away from the kiss and bite his lip. "Do you like how I ride you, killer?"

Grey puts both hands firmly on my hips to stop me from grinding on him.

Oops. I probably shouldn't have let my intrusive thoughts become outside words. In my head, I've been riding the face and fucking the dick of a cold, callous killer. He may not be cold and callous in reality, but he's still definitely a killer, even if he doesn't want to be.

"Sorry," I whisper.

He flips me onto my back on the bed, and his hands work down my shorts. The chain strains as he climbs between my legs. "Don't apologize," he growls before tugging his mask down.

He's the picture of what I've fantasized about. I've imagined this exact scenario, but it was a little less consensual. Sue me.

Grey sits up and spreads my legs wider. "You want this killer's dick? Every inch of it?"

"Please," I whimper.

He impales me on his cock as he pistons in and out of my poor pussy. I bite my lip to stop screaming, and he pins my arms above my head.

"I want you to fill me," I whimper, my voice growing hoarse.

"You want a big, bad killer to come inside you?"

I nod, much faster than I should. Embarrassingly so. I've never wanted anything more.

He wraps a hand around my throat, and like the slut I am, I lean into his grasp. I'm a breath away from saying "*Choke me, daddy*," but as if he read my mind, he squeezes and gives me a mind-numbing blood choke.

"Good little psycho," he whispers in my ear. His hips grow ragged, then stall as he fills me with warm heat.

He releases my arms and sits up on his knees as he pulls

the mask from his face. His dark hair sticks out in every direction, and that wild look still lingers in his eyes, but he turns from that menacing beast into the light Grey that I'm used to. He throws the mask beside my head and leans over me, then kisses me, soft and gentle. The act is so at odds with what we just did.

What he just did *to* me. God, it was so fucking hot.

"You have fucked-up fetishes," he says against my mouth.

"Don't kink shame me, asshole. I apologized. You're the one who went all-in with it. A big, bad killer, huh?"

"Shut your pretty mouth," he says before kissing me again. "Let's not talk about what just happened. I made you come, so you can't turn me in now."

We'll see about that. I still haven't decided what I plan to do with Grey, and now, I'm in no hurry to figure it out.

Chapter Ten

Grey

Guilt eats me from the inside the next morning as I sit across from Briar at the kitchen table. Each bite of pancake tastes horribly sour. Not even the diabetes-inducing syrup can help. Even so, I shovel each bite into my mouth. The sooner we finish eating, the sooner I can tap into that dead bitch's camera system.

"Is something bugging you?" Briar asks as she tidies up the dishes. "You've hardly spoken since . . . last night."

"Something about leg shackles doesn't exactly make me eager to converse in the mornings." I shift my feet around and rattle the chains. "Any chance we could try a trust exercise and let me walk around freely?"

Briar tightens her high ponytail and looks at my feet. "I guess we could try, but if you take off, I'll call the county sheriff."

If anyone should be contacting the county, it's me. I'm the one who's being held hostage in this really strange situation with this really strange woman who is starting to grow on me.

That's part of the problem. I liked what happened between us last night. It was dirty and wrong to play the killer in the bedroom, and I'm not playing. I am a killer. And she let me fill and fuck her until she was cross-eyed.

But what would my wife think? That's the question that keeps running through my mind, waving a banner. I run my finger over the place where my wedding band once rested. Now, that gold band rests with her and our unborn child in the casket.

"Do you still have your wedding ring?" Briar asks as she pulls the shackles from my ankles. "I only ask because I haven't seen it on your finger, but I sometimes notice you turning the place where it should be. My dad used to do that with his ring."

I shake my head and look out the window as the second shackle releases. "No, I don't have the ring anymore. Some habits die hard, I guess."

Briar sits back on her heels and looks up at me. "Would you ever remarry?"

"Never say never, but it's unlikely."

"I never want to get married. Sid did, but I wouldn't do it. I sure dodged one hell of a bullet there."

"Sid. Was that your ex with all the crazy fetishes?"

She nods. "Yeah, one and the same. I would have stayed loyal to that sorry piece of shit, with or without marriage, but he couldn't keep his dick in his pants. One night, I caught him with a couple of eighteen-year-olds. He thought I was off at a conference for medical billing specialists."

"Is that what you do for a living? You harass people about their medical bills?"

"Ouch, shots fired." She stands and stretches her lower

back. "Let's go to the living room. I want to see how high your reward is now."

I stand and follow her out of the kitchen. "We have an agreement, don't forget. I made you come, so you can't turn me in."

"Yeah, yeah." She flops on the couch and grabs the remote.

Light fills the screen, and she flips through the local channels until one of the stations finally airs their midday news segment. We sit through a story about a nursing home catching fire, another about a failing school system, and then some sports commentary. Finally, my face pops up in a small rectangle to the right of the news anchor's head.

"Police are still searching for the man who shot and killed bank CEO Gloria Rogers two days ago." Video taken outside the bank pops onto the television as the news anchor continues. She details the murder, then gives my description before finally saying, *"If anyone has any information, you're urged to contact the number on the screen. A reward has been offered for any tips that lead to an arrest and conviction."*

A number flashes on the screen, and Briar's jaw drops. "You're up to twenty grand, Grey! In two days, you've quadrupled the price on your head. How does it feel?"

It feels pretty shitty, if I'm being honest. I don't regret what I did, and if I had it to do over again, I'd make the same decisions. Every time I think about what I've done, I don't feel remorse. I feel pride.

What does that say about me?

"Now that the power's back, you can show me whatever it is you wanted me to see on the laptop." Briar rises from the couch and leaves the room. When she returns, she has a laptop in her hands. She places it on the coffee table, then connects the power cord. "It's old as dirt and won't turn on if it's not directly connected to a power source. The battery is shot."

She'll get no judgment from me. I haven't owned a laptop since the bank took everything but the car.

I pull the laptop in front of me and frown. "Do you have a VPN?"

She shakes her head. "What's that?"

"It stands for virtual private network. It basically encrypts your data, making it harder to track your digital footprint. Instead of entering websites head on and announcing your IP address at the front door, a VPN scoots you in through the back. I'd set you up, but I don't exactly have a method of payment."

She nibbles her lip and looks at a stack of envelopes on the table beside the door. "You think something in this footage will be the answer to both of our problems, right?"

I nod.

With a sigh, she goes to her bedroom and returns with a card in her hand. She holds it toward me. "Fucking charge it."

I pluck the card from her fingers and set to work. Within a few minutes, I've set up a secure connection and logged in to my secure accounts. I start by pulling the saved videos from the vault. If I want Briar on board with my plan, she needs to be made aware of a few things.

"There's something I want you to see." I turn the laptop so that the screen fully faces her. "When you're ready, hit play, but make sure you're ready. This isn't easy to watch."

Briar's eyebrows pull together, but she leans forward and hits play. I turn my head. The video was difficult to watch the first time, and the second time was torture, but I had to make sure I hadn't imagined what the camera captured. I don't need to see it a third time.

The sounds are enough to turn my stomach. A door creaks open in the video, and footsteps thump on expensive flooring. *"Is that fucking crayon on my wall, Doris? What did you do, you sorry little shit?"* a female voice slurs.

It's Gloria, and she's drunk. Doris is her adopted four-year-old daughter, and what Gloria thinks is crayon is actually a scuff from the movers mounting a picture in the hall. It took me all of three minutes to figure that out by going back just a few hours in the footage, but Mommy Dearest doesn't care where the mark came from. She's angry, and a four-year-old is a very easy target.

Briar slams the laptop shut after the first crack of the belt, and I don't blame her. This wasn't just a spanking. This was a full-on physical assault on a small child.

"I'm going to be sick," she says before rushing out of the room.

The reaction doesn't surprise me. I felt the same each time I watched that clip. The worst part? That video isn't the only proof of her depravity, and the little girl wasn't the only recipient of her unbridled rage.

The younger child, a mere infant, regularly screamed in his crib for hours. She probably wised up once the doctors started asking questions about the incessant rashes the baby developed from sitting in his own excrement for hours on end.

The dog she adopted from the shelter—an act which garnered a ton of publicity for the bank—met the most horrific fate of all. I won't go into the details, but let's just say that no living being can survive without food and water.

My original plan wasn't murder. When I cracked into her cameras, I had every intention of finding the skeletons in her closet and taking her down. I sent the videos of the abuse to news outlets, police departments, and anyone else with a listed address. No one responded, and it was swept under the rug.

That's what finally pushed me over the edge.

She took my wife and child from me. She took my home. There is no telling how many other lives she ruined. But when I outed her for the abuse of her children and the dog, nothing was done, so I had to do the right thing. When no one else cares, someone has to.

So I did.

Briar comes back into the room with a glass of water. She takes a sip, then sits beside me on the couch. "Sorry. That was more than I anticipated."

"It's understandable. I'd be more concerned if it didn't make you sick."

"No worries there." She holds the glass to her forehead and looks at the laptop. "I don't have to watch any more videos, do I? I can't handle seeing kids like that."

"We have more to see, but no more videos like that. Have a seat, and I'll lay out my plan."

Chapter Eleven

Grey

We've spent the last four hours poring over old footage revolving around one room in the house. In particular, one specific item: the safe. She kept it tucked away in the closet of her master bedroom, and one camera faces that closet. In each clip, she squats at a slightly different angle as she punches the numbers into the keypad, and we've almost cracked the code.

The plan after that is simple. Break into her mansion, crack the safe, and split whatever we find inside.

"Do you really think this could work?" Briar asks. "It sounds too simple."

I don't respond. I'm too busy watching her as she squints and leans closer to the screen as she rewatches a clip for the thousandth time. I should be focused on the task at hand, but that's difficult when my kidnapper/accomplice is so fucking hot.

Guilt rears its annoying head again. It reminds me that

I'm the reason my wife and I lost our home. That also means I'm the reason my wife and child are no longer alive. Happiness is something I don't deserve. It's something I will never deserve. Fucking Briar was a means to an end. I just went along with it so that she'll eventually let me go.

But as I look at her again, I know that isn't true. I fucked her because I wanted to. Yeah, she's borderline insane, but something about her brand of weird intrigues me instead of running me off. Her looks reel me in further.

The only thing holding me back is the memory of my wife.

"I think it's a five," Briar says. "She's definitely punching the middle of the keypad. It's too high up to be zero, and it's too low to be two. It's five or nine."

I scribble on the notepad. "So it looks like the code is two-seven-five or five-seven-five. Or maybe even two-seven-two. Does that sound right to you?"

"I'm not certain about the last number. It could be either." She nibbles her lip, and I have to look away. "How many tries do you think we'll get?"

"There's one way to find out." I pull the laptop in front of me and search for the safe's manufacturer. My answer appears after a few clicks. "We get three tries before we're locked out."

Briar flops back on the sofa and blows a few strands of auburn hair out of her face. "If we were only unsure of one number, that wouldn't be an issue, but two? We'd need at least four tries, and that's *if* we're certain about the other numbers."

She's starting to get antsy, and I can't have that. If I want to pull off this burglary, I need her help. I turn toward her and take her face into my hands.

"We will do this. Together. You're going to save your house, and I'm going to book a flight to a country that doesn't extradite." I lean closer so that her eyes are forced onto mine. "Look at me, Briar."

Her green eyes rise to mine, and whatever I planned to say goes right out of my head. Instead of talking, I lean closer and kiss her. At first, it's just a gut reaction to this contagious insanity. She's dangerous and beautiful, and I feel safest when I'm inside her, even though being inside her feels so wrong.

My dick hardens as her tongue presses against mine, asking for more. When I don't provide it, she grabs my hand and presses my fingertips between her legs with a soft moan against my mouth. I swallow her sounds and grind my fingers over her.

She pulls her mouth from mine and rolls her hips against my fingers. "Take off your pants, then don't stop touching me."

Like a siren issuing a command to a sailor, she demands things of me that I know I shouldn't do. Things that put my very life on the line. Because I can't stay. Even if we pull this off and we get more money than we know what to do with, she has ties to this land, and I need to cut all ties.

And even if she didn't have ties to the land, I have ties that won't break, no matter how I try to untangle myself from the past. I'll never be able to give this woman what she deserves, and I'll only hurt her in the end.

"If you knew this would only end in heartache, would you still do it?" I ask.

She huffs out a breath and rolls her eyes as she sits back. "If you don't want to fuck, you can just say so. There's no need to come up with silly excuses and reasons."

"Briar, that's not it. It's—"

"Your wife?"

Against my better judgment, I nod, then brace myself for a tirade. But Briar surprises me. Instead of launching into a jealous rage, she reaches out and takes my hand in hers.

"Look, I can't understand what happened with your wife unless you talk to me about it. Maybe if I know how Gloria caused your wife's death, I can at least try to understand, but you have to give me the opportunity."

I stare into my lap, at the calluses on the palms of my hands. My mouth forms the words, but I can't say them. I've never felt so weak in my life.

"Oh, for fuck's sake." Briar gets to her feet and leaves the room. When she returns, she's holding the ankle shackles in her hands. "I want to show you something. I want you to see . . ." She grits her teeth and looks at the ceiling, then takes a deep breath and looks at me. "I want to show you my deepest, darkest secret. But you have to wear these."

I look at the shackles. "Why?"

"Just . . . put them on. You just have to wear them. You'll understand why when we get there."

This seems like a pretty horrific omen of terrible things to come, but I fasten the ankle shackles to my legs anyway.

"You'll need your boots. We have to go into the woods for this." She drops my shoes at my shackled feet. "Once I show you this, you can also trust that I won't turn you in. It's pretty damning, and it explains why I can't lose this property."

A cold sweat slicks my palms as I tie my laces. What could be so horrible that it would cause her to go to drastic measures to keep this land? I figured it was just a sentimental attachment, but the way she's talking, this goes deeper than that.

Despite my growing unease, I stand and follow her out the front door. As the sun dips lower in the sky, we walk into the woods.

Chapter Twelve

Briar

This is a horrible idea, and I don't know what I'm thinking by bringing him out here. It's the act of a desperate woman, I guess. He still doesn't trust me, and if I want him to bring his secrets into the light, he'll need to.

And who better to tell my secret to than a murderer? It's not like he can go to the cops with this information. Sure, he could probably use what I'm about to show him to finagle some sort of plea deal, but it's not likely.

My victim wasn't exactly adored by the public, after all.

We reach the tilted shed that stands beside a crumbling chimney. It's all that's left of the small house that one stood on this plot of land. The shed was actually a pantry. It was an addition to the house, and aside from the chimney, it's the only thing that remains.

I step forward and pull open the wooden door. Its rusted hinges don't squeak, though. They groan, complaining about their years of service and wishing for death. I felt that way once, but instead of killing myself, I took out the source of my misery.

"Grey, I'd like you to meet Sid."

Instead of stepping forward and taking a look inside, Grey turns his head and vomits in the scrub. The response is valid. I'm not an embalmer, and Sid has been rotting in this shed for weeks. The smell is pretty horrible.

Grey wipes his mouth on the sleeve of his coat. "Did you do that? I mean . . . What the fuck happened to him?"

"I killed him." I lift my shoulders in a shrug. "After years of mental abuse shifted into physical torture, I snapped."

Grey peers into the shed, then closes his eyes. "What about the two girls?"

My eyes widen. "Oh, no! I didn't kill him when I found him with the girls, and I damn sure wouldn't hurt two naïve children who were swayed by a perv. I was—"

Before I can finish my sentence, my throat closes off. I swallow and try to start again, but now I'm crying. The emotions overtake me before I realize what's happening, and I can't tell him the catalyst. I can't voice the loss that spurred me to stab him as he slept.

Now would be the perfect time for him to run, but he doesn't. He steps closer and pulls me into him, and I wail against his chest. This wasn't how this was supposed to go. Sid's loss doesn't affect me, and it never has. It never will. The loss that hurts the most is one I try to pretend doesn't exist.

But it did. It did exist.

"You were pregnant," he whispers against the top of my head, and I nod. I can't speak those words again. The one person I told was the same person who took that from me.

"I knew for a total of three hours before he beat me until

I lost—" My throat clamps down again. "The scars are still all over my body. You understand, don't you? You know why I had to do it?"

"More than you know."

"Then explain it to me. How do you know, Grey? I've laid everything out for you, and now I want you to do the same."

"Briar . . . I can't."

"Tell me!"

"No!"

A cold emptiness embraces me as he releases his hold and takes a step back. Tears brim in his eyes, but he doesn't allow them to fall.

"What more do you need from me?" I ask. I reach down and rip off my shirt. "Do you need to see the scars? Will that help you understand that I'm damaged too?" I kick off my pants and stand in the freezing woods in nothing more than my underwear. "Look at them! Look at the scars, Grey."

He keeps his head turned, refusing to witness the proof of what I've been through.

"These are the scars you can see, but there are others that—"

"Do you think I don't know that? You can't see any of my scars, but they cut deep. My wife killed herself, Briar, and she took our baby with her. When we lost the house, she saw no hope. Gloria took that from us, just like she took my wife and child. That's why I killed her. She had to pay for the lives she stole from me, with *fucking interest*!"

We stare at each other, our chests heaving up and down as we share a cathartic moment in the woods. Just two murderers, airing out their grievances. Completely normal.

My shoulders relax, and I take a step toward him. "Fuck, I'm sorry. I shouldn't have pushed you."

He raises his hands to keep me from getting any closer. Then he turns and starts toward the house.

I gather my clothes and dress before following him. The shackles weren't needed. He isn't going anywhere until we get the money, and if we get the money, I'm saved as well. I should feel so much better right now. I have everything I wanted. Safety. His secrets.

So why do I feel like I have nothing at all?

Chapter Thirteen

Briar

The next few weeks pass in a whirlwind. Because I didn't have a lot of time saved up, I was forced to return to work. The first few days were scary. Each time I returned home, I expected to find the couch empty and his things gone. After the first week, I finally started to relax.

We've been watching the cams every day. The feed comes complete with audio, so the meetings between the lawyers and Gloria's sister—who is tapped to inherit her estate and children—have provided tons of information. Our greatest fear was that the sister would break into the safe and take any valuables before we had a chance to formulate a plan, but she seems to be the complete opposite of Gloria in every possible way. Instead of combing the house for financial gain, she's devoted most of her time to the children.

That's good for them, and Grey and I have both discussed how his actions have actually made their lives better. Even though he didn't kill her for their sakes, they still reaped the benefits. I would never speak this thought aloud, but I like to imagine that those two children are our way of ensuring the babies who were stolen from us get to live on.

As for the relationship between me and Grey, I don't know where we stand. We haven't had sex since that one night, but the longing looks are there. Sometimes I catch him watching me out of the corner of my eye, but I'm thankful he hasn't caught me watching him.

In the shower.

When he's sleeping.

Once when he was beating his dick while standing in front of the sink.

I'm not proud of myself, but I've developed a bit of an obsession. Too bad it isn't reciprocated. I fucked that up when I pushed him to talk.

Things have been different since that moment in the woods. I expected him to be weirded out or possibly scared of me after learning I murdered my ex, but I've been the one pussyfooting around. I don't want to lose him, even though that's the end goal. After we complete the job next week, he'll hop on a plane and fly to safety.

"Nothing's changed, has it?" I say as I set a steaming mug of decaf coffee in front of him at the kitchen table. "I mean, she's still planning to take the kids out of town for a few days, right?"

Grey taps the computer screen. "That painting has been moved. Look at it."

My eyebrows pull together as I look at the image. This camera points down a hallway, at the end of which hangs a massive painting of a black butterfly. The gold frame looks mildly askew, but I'm not sure why that matters.

"Maybe someone bumped it," I offer, but Grey shakes his head and taps the screen again.

"I thought that too, but when I went back through the footage from earlier today, I realized we're missing a chunk of time. Someone patched in footage from a different video from three p.m. to three fifteen."

"Who would do that? And why?"

He leans closer to the screen. "That's the question, isn't it?"

I sit in a chair and scoot closer so that I can see the screen as well. Our shoulders touch, but he doesn't seem to mind. Meanwhile, I revel in the closeness. His nose twitches, and he turns his head to face me.

"You, um . . . you smell nice."

I smile at him. "Thanks."

This is what we've been reduced to. Awkward compliments and stolen glances.

"New perfume?" he asks.

"No. I tried a new lotion, but I think it's drying out my skin." I hold my arm toward him, and he runs his fingertips over the fine reddish-blonde hairs.

"Feels pretty soft to me." He swallows, then clears his throat. "It smells good too."

"You said that already."

"Right."

I scoot my chair away so that we aren't touching. Apparently, being too close to him scrambles his fucking brain. I'd have considered it a compliment, my ability to intimidate a murderer, but I don't want to intimidate him. I want to seduce him.

"I know the job is still a week out and we're supposed to focus, but I'm struggling with that," I say. "Can we talk about this?"

"What? The job? Yeah, of course."

"No, Grey. Not the job." I grip the seat of his chair and spin him away from the laptop so that he's forced to look at me. "I'm sorry I essentially forced you to talk about what happened, but that was weeks ago. Will you ever let it go?"

His dark eyebrows pull together, and he looks more confused than I feel. "Let it go? I'm not holding on to anything."

I take his hand and place it on my breast, and he pulls away as if I've held his palm against a blazing stovetop.

"See!" I shout. "My tits weren't so undesirable to you before. Now we walk around and pretend we don't have the hots for each other when we very clearly do. What gives?"

"I don't want to . . ." He stops and shakes his head. "Is that what you want? What you *really* want? You want the man, the complete idiot who signed for a loan and failed to keep his house . . . That's the man you want inside you? The failure?"

I nod my head. "In a nutshell, yes. Why is this so hard for you to understand?"

"It's not hard for me to understand, but we can't be anything. Haven't you thought about that? About what happens when we get the money and go our separate ways?"

"No, not really. I'm more of a here-and-now kind of girl. I don't really think too far ahead. That's how I've ended up with mountains of debt, an impending foreclosure, and a dead ex-boyfriend in the woods. Foresight ain't my strong suit, dude."

"Then think about it now," he says. "I don't want to hurt you, Briar, and that's what I'll do if I leave you after I get the money. And I can't stay."

He's right. I really haven't thought about any of that.

Rationally, I know his plan has always been to get out of here, but I've never really thought about what that looks like for me, the woman who's plan has always been to dig in and stay put.

"Yeah, you're right. It's going to hurt like hell when you leave. I like you, and I'm not afraid to admit it." I stand and grip the hem of my shirt, then remove it. "It's a pain I'm willing to endure for a moment of pleasure, though." I grip my pants and lower them. "What about you, Grey? Is the pleasure worth the pain it causes you?"

He bites his bottom lip and groans as I drop into my chair, spread my legs, and rub my clit through my panties.

"Touch me," I whisper. "Make me feel good before you hurt me. If you have to leave, then give me something to remember you by."

"Psycho," he whispers.

He wants me. I know he does. *He* knows he does. But something keeps him from admitting it. If it's his wife, we all have a skeleton. Mine just lives in the backyard.

Then I remember the mask. It helped him before, so maybe it can help him again. I hurry to the bedroom and grab it, then return to the kitchen. Realizing what I hold, he walks over and snatches the fabric from my hand, then puts it on. He takes off his shirt and boxes me in with his strong arms. The tattoos stare back at me. Delinquent. Foreclosure. Everything I've felt so intimately myself. It's as if they're etched into my own skin.

"No matter how much I want to, you can't convince me to stay. I've been fighting this every day. Being around you is torture, and I don't want to be weak." He turns me around and pulls me against his body until his erection grinds against my ass. "But fuck if you don't make me weak."

I look back and smirk at him. "Would a weak person commit homicide?"

"Maybe." He lifts a hand to my face and raises my chin before his fingers trail down my neck. He squeezes my throat. "I could kill you right now, little psycho."

"But you won't."

His pants fall to the floor, and he rips my panties down my thighs. He bends me over the table as his warm, silky cock brushes against my wet slit. He draws back his hips, then pushes inside me on my next inward breath. Fuck, he feels so big from this angle.

"Grey," I moan.

The table scoots forward as he pounds into me. Once the wooden edge hits the wall and can't move forward anymore, he puts all that strength through me instead. Every collision of his hips drives me into the table's edge.

Grey is a kind, broken man, but when he puts on that mask, he's someone else entirely. Someone capable of the ultimate sin. That's all I can think about as he reaches around and squeezes my throat.

My brain goes to weird places, like him actually killing me. Keeping me as some weird sex doll he can selfishly use whenever he wants. I want him to be *that* obsessed with me. As obsessed as I am with him. I would keep his body around too. Not for sex, but to talk about my day with and share stories with until he rots away in my bed.

He's bad for me. I'm bad for him. And I know damn well that we can't stay together after this.

"Come back to me, little psycho," he says. "Whatever you're thinking about, stop it."

He wraps his arm around my chest and pulls me upright. With one swipe of his powerful arm, he moves the table out of the way and walks me against the wall. I spin in his hold, and his hands lift my thighs and wrap them around his waist. He pulls me out of my mental gymnastics as he pushes himself into me and forces me to look into his beautiful eyes as he rails me.

His fingertips dig into my ass, and his grunts and groans make the walls of my pussy spasm and tighten. His hand drops between us, and he rubs my clit in tight circles. Fuck, it's electric. The pleasure vibrates the length of my spine as he brings me close to another orgasm.

"I want you to come on my cock again, little psycho. Squeeze every drop from a killer's dick."

His fingers work me until I rocket skyward. I scream out as more inhuman sounds wrench from me. My eyes clamp shut, and I lose all control of my body. Every muscle tightens and tenses and pulls a groan from him. He's coming too, and the stuttering roughness of his hips intensifies.

I'll get off to this moment for many nights to come.

We finally stop coming, and he pulls his twitching dick from me, then raises the mask. He kisses me as if he's been waiting this entire time to do exactly that. As if he didn't want to ruin this moment by shedding his dark identity.

"What were you thinking about before?" he asks, his wet cock resting against my pussy.

"What it will be like when you leave," I whisper.

He sighs and strokes my hair, and yes, he's firmly out of his morally gray role now. "You know we can't stay together."

"Why? We're both killers. What does it matter?"

"Because my murder was very public, and the entire state is looking for me."

"Based on the internet, the entire world is looking for you, actually. But not in the way you think."

"Okay, but the people who *are* trying to find me for

murder will lead the police right to your door. And because you're a *little bit* psychotic, you have a body in the backyard. Me staying around isn't good for either of us. You wanted me to give you something to remember me by, and I did, just as you asked. You will remember my touch. My kiss. My cock. Unless, of course, you think we should stop this now to avoid any further pain."

"Call me a glutton for punishment, I guess, because I want to eat up every moment of my future pain. Right here. Right now."

"Then I'll keep feeding you until you can't hold another drop of me." He leans down and kisses me, but another thought circles my brain.

He can't stay here, but who's to say I can't go with him?

I smile and deepen the kiss. Once we have the money, I'll tell him my plan. I don't know how he'll take it. There's every chance that the obsession is one-sided and he's only fucking me as a way to pass the time until he takes off. There's every chance that he plans to fuck me over once he gets the cash.

For now, I'll just have to keep trusting him.

Chapter Fourteen

Grey

The past few days have been filled with plans for the upcoming job, but we occasionally take breaks to eat, sleep, and watch the news. And fuck. We make lots of time for that, and I've taken Briar in nearly every room of the house at every time of day. The woman has a sexual hunger rivaled by none, and I'm her favorite restaurant, apparently. Which is fine, as she's become mine as well.

The woman in my grasp has morphed into something different. Something I absolutely cannot kill, even to my own detriment. There's too much of an understanding between us now. Something deeper than her holding me captive for no reason. I know the reasons now, and instead of pushing me away, they've forced me to admit something to myself.

She and I are kindred spirits.

Fate forced our hands, and now we are two pariahs who no longer fit with society. We're emotionally fucked, for lack of a better term. It's a shame we can't stick together after this, but our decision to part ways after we get the money is the right call.

"Looks like you're capping out at fifty grand," Briar says as she enters the bedroom with a tray in her hands. She places it on the bed and looks at me. "We'll get more than that from her safe, right?"

"That bitch probably spent fifty grand on a daily basis," I say with a scoff. "If we find less than that in the safe, I'll give it all to you and turn myself in."

She plucks a strawberry from the tray of fruit and chews it as she mulls over my words. "If it ends up like that, I don't need all of it. I only need enough to straighten out my mortgage and get ahead. And maybe pay off a little credit card debt. My car was making a funny sound on my way home from work, though . . ."

"It truly never ends, does it?" I lean forward and grab a few blueberries, then pop them into my mouth. "The bills, I mean. We spend our entire lives owing somebody something."

My black mask falls into my lap. When I look up at Briar, she's smirking.

"Grey, it has come to our attention that you have a past due balance. To avoid legal action, please make a deposit at our nearest facility." She slaps her pussy and smiles at me.

I look down at the mask. It makes everything possible for me, and I can't fuck her without it. When I wear it, I'm not the man with a dead wife and child. I'm the killer who took down an evil, greedy, abusive woman. Those lifetimes didn't exist together, so it's a way to separate myself.

It's a way to remain faithful to my dead wife.

But then I look up at Briar. I want to give her all of me. I want to fuck her without wearing the mask. Why is that so difficult for me?

I pluck up the mask and spin it around my finger as I enjoy a chunk of banana. "We still need to go over the plan one more time. I want to be sure we both understand our parts."

Briar strips off her shirt, tempting me as she lies back in nothing more than a bra and some silky sleep shorts. "I'll be at home, watching the cameras to keep you safe. You'll be at the mansion, going through the safe and collecting the money. There. Can we fuck now?"

She spreads her legs and squeezes her mound through the thin shorts. A low moan eases out of her, and the blood rushes to my cock. My cock does nothing with it, though. If I want to fuck her, I'll need to wear the mask.

"Put it on," she begs. "Once you make me come again, I'll pay attention and be a good girl. I promise."

The woman is insatiable, and it's such a fucking turn on. She can't get enough of me, and the feeling is reciprocated. If I could just fuck her without the mask . . .

But I can't, so I give in and slide the scratchy fabric over my face.

The erection is nearly instantaneous. Grey is gone, replaced by a man who is safe to ravage the beautiful woman in front of him. The desperate killer has no ties to a past. Hell, he doesn't have ties to a future. He's connected only to the woman who desires him fully, and that woman is right now. That woman is Briar.

"I want you to do something for me, Grey," she says, looking up at me.

"What?"

She leans over, pulls something from a drawer within her bedside table, and walks over to me. What she puts in my hand surprises me.

It's my gun.

Briar sits on the bed. Her fingers trace the black metal, almost lovingly. If she wants me to kill her, she's chosen the wrong person for the job. Even with my mask on, I couldn't do it. I hate to admit it, but I actually like having her around.

"I want you to fuck me with it," she says.

I rip off the mask. "Excuse me?"

"I want you to put the barrel inside me."

"There are so many safety reasons that—"

"I don't care."

"I do!"

But then she nibbles her bottom lip, and I care a little less. And when she lifts her legs and spreads her thighs, I care not at all.

With a groan, I pull the mask over my face as she moves the crotch of her shorts aside, exposing her sweet little slit. It begs to be filled, but she doesn't want my cock this time. No, she wants a murder weapon inside her.

My murder weapon.

I make a move to unload the pistol because I'm not stupid, but she puts her hand over mine, silently asking me to leave it loaded. While I don't particularly want to play Russian roulette with Briar's body, if that's what she wants, I'll play.

I steel myself, then drag the metal barrel down the curves of her belly and between the lips of her pussy. She drops her head back as I rub her with the rough metal, then drag it downward and push it inside her. She gasps as the small front sight slips past her opening. Her inner lips spread around the barrel, and I'm in awe. It's not often that I get to witness perfection from this angle. The greed of her pussy. Every inch being taken and released.

"Fuck me," she pants.

Her back arches as I piston the gun inside her, and I can't deny the flare of jealousy I feel for the chunk of metal in my hand. I want to be that gun.

The mattress creaks beneath me as I get onto my knees and lean over her. My hand rises to her throat and squeezes, and her irises roll toward the back of her head. She tightens around the barrel. Her thighs tremble. She spasms as pleasure drips down the metal and heads toward my skin.

"Fuck, you're so pretty, little psycho," I growl. "Even prettier when you're about to come."

"Grey," she pants.

Her mouth opens and closes as my words hit her right between her legs. Her chest rises into mine, and she comes around the barrel of my gun. I raise my mask toward my nose because I *need* to inhale her moans. I need to devour them.

I kiss her before pulling the barrel from her pussy and bringing it to her chin. "Open your mouth, psycho, and taste yourself on my gun."

I shove the wet barrel past her lips, then lean forward and lick her come off my hand. When a groan eases out of me, her lips tighten around the barrel. She tastes like the sin I committed, and I eat it up. I want more of it. Her sweetness washes away the metallic taste of the blood I've spilled.

I push the barrel deeper into her mouth and release my cock from my pants with my other hand. I can't wait a moment longer to feel her warm, come-soaked pussy around my dick.

"I want you to choke on my pistol. I want to fuck your throat with this gun while you take my cock in your greedy pussy. You want more, don't you?"

She nods.

Making sure my finger is far away from the trigger, I

grip my dick and push inside her. She gasps around the gun. I fuck her throat with the barrel as I rail her pussy, and the sight is almost too much. Her tits bounce with every thrust of my hips, and her throat tenses and extends.

"Such a good fucking psycho," I grit out.

Her moans filter past the intrusion, and I become desperate for them. They need to reach my ears without anything between, so I pull the gun from her mouth and set it on the bedside table. I fist her hair and pull her against me as I fuck her harder. Faster. Until she's screaming out my name and I'm desperate to fill her. My hand glides down her soft skin and grips her ass as I pull her closer. She's flush against me now, her warm wetness dripping and soaking me.

"Please! Fill me!" she screams.

I place my hand over her mouth, lean my weight into her, and selfishly use her body in ways I didn't even know I was capable of. I didn't know I was capable of a lot of things until recently. My hips stutter and my tempo slows as I fill her pussy. My dick twitches as an intense orgasm encompasses my entire body.

I roll to the side and lie beside her with a thick coating of sweat on my skin. For a moment, the lines blur as she leans over me, pulls off the mask, and kisses me. I'm both the killer and Grey, and I don't know how to rationalize those two worlds existing in the same space. And I can't even begin to try, for her sake.

Because once I get the cash, it won't matter anymore. This time tomorrow, I'll be worlds away.

Chapter Fifteen

Briar

Taking his car anywhere would be a death sentence, so using my car, I drive him about a mile from the mansion and drop him off. No words pass between us as he exits the vehicle. Anything we needed to say has already been said.

After shutting the car door, he slips into the thick wooded area beside the road. I cut on the interior light and pretend to look for something in the center console. This is all an act in case someone spots my car. They'll remember seeing a lone woman and nothing more.

When enough time has passed and at least three cars have driven by, I glance into the dark woods and find him hunkered down behind a large tree trunk and a few thick bushes. I nod toward him, and he nods back, signaling that we're ready to do what needs to be done. With a flick of my fingers, I cut off the dome light, then pull onto the road.

He'll wait in the brush until I get back to the house and call him. He didn't have a cell phone, so that meant he had to use mine. I'll use my laptop to communicate with him while he's in the house. I'll be his eyes.

The mansion should be empty for a few days—Gloria's kind sister took the kids away for the weekend, exactly as planned—but I'm not taking any chances. Especially not when someone else is already tweaking the footage. Whoever cut the section from the video doesn't know who is watching, but they know that someone is, and that makes me nervous.

Thirty minutes later, I pull into my driveway and hurry into the house. It was weird to leave him at the house while I've been going to work, but it's even stranger to enter my bedroom and not see him sprawled across the bed, wearing his little metal collar. It's an absence I'll need to get used to. He might dick me down one final time before he takes off, but when the sun rises tomorrow morning, he'll be a distant memory.

I thought I'd be fine with this arrangement. Not many women would relish the idea of tying themselves to a murderer for the rest of their lives, but maybe those women aren't also killers. Waking up to him every morning wouldn't have been the worst change in my life.

I understand why he can't stay, though. With such a memorable face, he'd be discovered in no time. Leaving with him is another option, but he hasn't asked me to join him. If he did, I would definitely say yes, but I can't just insert myself into whatever he has planned after this. If he still hasn't said anything before he leaves, I'll drop a hint.

With my computer in hand, I hurry to the kitchen table and begin setting everything up. None of these fantasies and plans will amount to anything at all if we don't get that money. Before booting up the feed to the security cameras, I call Grey. He answers on the second ring.

"Can you hear me, psycho?" he asks.

I nod, even though he can't see me. "Loud and clear, killer."

"Good." Something crunches, and he drops his voice to a whisper. "I'm still in the woods, but I should be nearing the back of the property now. Can you pull up the feed that shows the back lawn?"

After a few keystrokes, I'm in. "I'm watching now," I say as I study the screen. It shows the sprawling grass and a corner of the back porch.

"Any movement?"

I click another camera view, then another. "I don't see any movement or lights in the house. Do you want me to do a full sweep?"

He grunts, then says, "Yeah, might as well. The brush just thickened up, and I may have to take the long way around anyway."

I click through the different camera views as his breath and footsteps occasionally come through the laptop speakers. Everything looks ideal. The large rooms are dark and empty, and the house is quiet.

"There aren't any hidden surprises that I can see. The alarm is armed, but we expected that," I say. "You still remember the alarm code for the back door, right?"

"One-two-three-four," he grunts, and a shadowy figure appears on the screen overlooking the backyard.

His shadowy figure.

As I watch him slink across the grass, I have never been more turned on. He's like my own personal Robin Hood, stealing from the egregiously wealthy to help out poor little old me. Granted, he's lining his own pockets as well, but that's beside the point. He doesn't have to give me any of it, yet he plans to share it.

"I have a visual," I say, and he waves at one of the cameras. "Wrong way. Turn toward the south."

He turns and faces the camera I'm watching, and my thighs rub together. His eyes look back at me through the hole in his balaclava, and I can only think of the moments we've shared while he wore that mask. I hope he plans to fuck me one more time while wearing it. It won't be enough, and I'll always long for more, but it's better than knowing our last time was our last time.

"Let's get this shit show on the road," he says.

I switch the camera to the interior shot that shows the back door. Seconds later, Grey hurries inside and disables the alarm. We've seen this room so many times from this high vantage point, so it must be disorienting for him now. He turns in a tight circle and tries to get his bearings.

"The room you need is down that long hall to the right," I say, and he nods.

As he wanders through the maze of hallways and eventually finds the bedroom, I click through the cameras and follow his journey, only speaking up when he seems lost. When he finally reaches the closet, I hold my breath.

He opens the door and steps into the deep room that could likely double as sleeping quarters. With the speed of a snail, he steps toward the massive black box sitting on the carpet. I grip the edge of the table and nibble my bottom lip as he squats and punches in the first code, which must be incorrect, because he looks up at the ceiling and shakes out his hands before trying again.

This time, the safe clicks open.

"Jackpot," he whispers. But instead of hurriedly shoving piles of cash into the black bag dangling from his shoulder, he pulls a single slip of paper from the safe and begins reading it.

"Grey, what does it say?" I ask. "Is it a will or something? What is it?"

"I don't know what to make of this," he says. On the screen, he goes to stand, and I can finally see inside the safe.

It's empty.

"What does the paper say?" I scream at the screen. "What is happening?"

Grey faces the camera and fluffs the paper before reading aloud. "I was hoping you'd come for this, but I had to move it to keep it safe. You gave the children freedom, and now I want to give the same to you. Fly high, vigilante."

I wait for him to continue, but he doesn't. He just folds the paper, stuffs it into his pocket, and stands beside the bed.

"So that's it?" I finally say. "It's over. I can't save my house, and you can't run off to Mexico to catch the next flight to China."

Grey blows out a breath. "I wouldn't have enjoyed China anyway. I speak neither Mandarin nor Cantonese."

"Wait, wait. Back up. Read that note again."

He pulls it out and reads it again, and I hear what I thought I remembered.

"They said they had to move it. What about the painting?" I click through the cameras until I land on the long hall. "Leave that room and take a left, then take the next right."

A few seconds later, Grey appears on the screen. "They said to fly high, so maybe they were trying to nudge me toward the painting."

"Exactly," I say as I allow hope to rise.

Holding my breath once more, I watch as Grey creeps closer to the painting. The massive gold frame still hangs at an almost imperceptible off-kilter angle. It's too big for any one person to lift, so I don't know how he'll get it down from the wall.

But then he doesn't have to. As he grips the frame, I'm the image of astonishment as it spins on the wall and becomes a door. He looks back at the camera once more, then grips the frame and opens the wall.

That's when the camera feed cuts out, and the screen displays an error message.

Chapter Sixteen

Briar

It's been forty-eight hours, and I think it's time I admit defeat. He isn't coming back. My bigger concern should be losing my house and having my crimes brought to light, but that isn't what has me so gutted. It's that I trusted him. I cared about him. And just like Sid, he fucked me over.

Out of obsessive compulsion, I check the camera feed for the fortieth time today. Nothing has changed. The butterfly painting is back in its correct orientation, but it's been that way since the feed came back an hour after going down.

I tried tracing my phone, but it's been turned off since the cameras went offline. Because of the exact timing of the total technology crash, I can only assume something jammed all the signals going in or out of that house. At first, I thought the feds had captured him, but something would have been on the news by now, and he's not even mentioned anymore.

That can only mean one thing. Yes, the total disconnect

was planned, but not by the feds. This was all orchestrated by Grey. All along, he was just using me as a place to crash until he got his shit together. That was the plan from the beginning, sure, but I was also included in the endgame. My needs were considered—or so I thought. Somewhere along the way, he changed his mind about sharing the money.

I close the laptop and tell myself I don't care, that none of this matters anyway. Nothing has changed. I'm still in the same position I was in before I met him. The hole in my heart is a little larger, sure, but life is just as hopeless as it ever was.

But no matter how many times I repeat this new mantra, I can't make myself believe it. He didn't just take the money. He took a part of me when he ran off. I gave him that part of myself, thinking it didn't matter, but it does. It matters so fucking much. The part that he took with him was my last shred of hope for a future that doesn't involve a jail cell or permanent solitude.

I stand from the kitchen table and meander toward the bathroom, where I run a tub full of warm water. I dump in the last of a rose-scented bath oil that's supposed to soften my skin. My skin should be pretty soft by the time I'm found. That's if it's still attached to my body.

After placing three razor blades on the lip of the tub, I remove my clothes. I fold each garment into a neat cube and place it on the closed toilet seat. When I'm discovered, I don't want anyone to think I was a slob. Not that it will matter much once they find the dead body in the woods. Then again, I wouldn't want anyone to think I killed myself because of pining for that piece of shit. Maybe I need to make sure my voice is heard once I'm gone.

Naked, I hurry to the living room and go straight for the desk drawer where I keep a pad of paper and some chewed pencils. I spend the next forty-five minutes drawing up a suicide note that explains why I had to do this, though it's specially curated to only reveal what I want to reveal.

That I'm so far behind on my mortgage payments that I see no way to keep my house.

That I killed a man who abused me emotionally and physically, and I see no way to make a jury of my peers understand that.

I see no way. That's the common thread here. That's what my letter says. I see no way, so I'm stopping the journey here. I want off the ride now.

The letter doesn't include anything about Grey. I left him out because if there is any chance he escaped, I don't just want him to survive. Despite everything, despite fucking me over, I want him to thrive. A mention in a suicide note might give them the tip they need.

Then again, there's a shitload of evidence on my computer, plus the entire car in my garage, and both things will tie him back to me. Hell, the media might even find a way to spin this that blames him for my death, and I can't have that.

The suicide note flutters from my hand and falls to the floor. Fuck, there is no way to do this that doesn't potentially tie Grey back to me. I've been too rash. Before I off myself, I need to ensure any trace of Grey is wiped from my home.

I hurry to my computer, then begin factory-resetting everything. My phone can't be helped, but nothing terribly incriminating would have been on it. Nothing that would harm Grey, anyway. As that's busy removing all trace of activity, I go to the bedroom to dress. I'll need to get rid of the car, and I can't do that in my birthday suit.

Getting rid of Grey's car won't be that difficult. The cops already saw it turn down this road, so when they eventually find it in the abandoned barn a mile away, it won't seem that crazy. Once I drop it off, I'll hurry back here and . . . Well, I'll do what I need to do.

This isn't my first choice, but it's my final choice. I'm left with no other options. Grey was my last hope of anything. When he took that money and ran, he took any chance I had of ever having an ending other than a jail cell or a grave.

I want to be angry with Grey. As I pull on my pants, then fasten my bra, I search deep inside myself for some rage or indignation. He was the one who offered me hope and pulled it away. But I only feel sad.

I grab Grey's car keys from the kitchen drawer. I tucked them there after parking his car in my garage. He could have easily found them and taken off, but he had to hang around for that money.

He certainly didn't hang around for me. I know that now.

I'm about to step into the garage when a thought crosses my mind. Though I've completely wiped the computer, all the data can probably be retrieved if someone wants it badly enough. When they find the dead body in the woods, that will certainly up their drive for answers. Maybe I should burn it . . .

And maybe I'm just procrastinating because I really don't want to die. I just don't want to live anymore.

With a huff, I snatch up the computer—and all those polaroids, sketches, and printouts of Grey—and trudge into the backyard. I walk until I'm far enough from the house that I don't fear a stray wind carrying an ember onto the property and burning the structure to the ground. While that's not the worst idea, I would prefer to buy Grey a little more time, just in case I've forgotten anything else that might incriminate him.

I don't know why I'm still protecting him, but I want him to escape. In some weird way, if he makes it, we all make it. He'll carry a little piece of everyone who's been fucked over by the rich.

I drag the burn barrel over from the side of the house and drop some wood into the bottom. After dumping the laptop inside, I hurry into the house and grab Grey's clothes. Anything he's worn in the weeks he's been here goes into my arms, where I tote everything outside and drop it on top of the computer. I douse everything in lighter fluid, then toss a match onto the pile.

Flames burst from the barrel, and I take a step back. That's when I hear the guttural scream from inside the house.

Chapter Seventeen

Grey

The suicide note crumples in my fist as I drop to my knees in Briar's living room. I was afraid she would think I'd abandoned her, but I never imagined she felt this hopeless. I never imagined I would be faced with a repeat of the past.

A high-pitched whine joins the beat of my heart in my ears. My vision goes hazy, and I feel like I might vomit. My wife didn't leave a note, but this situation is still too similar. Too familiar.

My stomach rolls as I recall finding my wife in the bathroom. But in that vision, her face becomes Briar's. My wife's blonde hair floats on the water, shifting from brown to auburn. The blood is still red, though. So much blood.

I close my eyes and will the mental images away with another roaring scream. What I feel for Briar isn't love, but it could have been. With time and care, it could have been so much more. She's strange and beautiful, and I wanted nothing more than to hold her in my arms one final time and ask her—

"Grey?"

I scramble to stand and turn around. My ankle bumps against the coffee table's leg, but I can't even scream in pain as my eyes land on a ghost.

"Briar? I thought you . . ." I unclench my fist and look at the note again.

She rushes forward and snatches the note from my hand. "Fuck whatever you thought. You have to get out of here! You should be in China right now."

I grip her shoulders. "Promise me you won't do that. Promise me right fucking now."

"Grey—"

"Promise me!" I shake her shoulders and stare into her green eyes. "Nobody ever gives me the time to figure shit out. They always jump straight to the nearest fucking exit. Promise me that you will *never* step toward the exit again, Briar, or I will call the cops and turn myself in right fucking now."

Her knees wobble, and she collapses to the couch. She's unable to look at me as tears fill her eyes. "What was I supposed to do? What was I supposed to do when I thought you ran off with the last of any chance I had at a life?"

"You keep living. That's what you do." I step closer and kneel in front of her, then take her hands in mine. "You don't live for a man. You don't live for a house or your freedom. You don't live for anything other than Briar. No matter what happens, you have to promise me you'll keep living. Be a thorn in someone's side, little psycho, even if it's not mine."

She finally meets my gaze. "But what am I supposed to

do? There is an entire dead person in the woods behind my house. I am about to lose said house, at which point, the body will be discovered. To top everything off, the best relationship I've ever had is with a murderer who is about to leave my life forever."

"Not if you come with me." I smile up at her. "I have so much to tell you."

As we stand beside the burn barrel, I explain everything that's happened since the tech crash during the burglary. It turned out that someone suspected we were watching the cameras, and we were just lucky that this person was on my side.

The bank bitch's depravity was much deeper and wider than we realized. The children weren't just abused in her care. They were exploited as well. Beverly—Gloria's sister—had been trying to get authorities to listen for months, but no one would hear her. When I killed Gloria, I finally brought her evil deeds to light, and as thanks, Beverly put aside the money in the safe. The money Gloria had been using to pay people to turn a blind eye would now go to me.

And then some.

When Beverly ended the camera feed and the phone signal, she told me everything, gave me the money, and took me to a secure location. Once there, she used some of her contacts to fabricate a couple of passports and buy some first-class tickets to Russia. She knows of a small expat village there where we'll be safe.

"We?" Briar asks. "You want me to come with you?"

I pull the passports from my pocket and hand them to her. "That's why I was gone for so long. I couldn't contact you because Beverly insisted I destroy your phone so nothing could be traced to either of us."

"What if I don't want to go?" She studies the passport that displays her face, accompanied by information fabricated by Beverly. Then she looks up at me. "What if I want to stay here?"

There was always a possibility that she wouldn't come with me, but I didn't expect this to be her response, which means I didn't expect my chest to ache viscerally with this response, either.

I pull a metal card from my coat pocket and hand it to her. "If you don't want to come with me, you can have all the money. That card is connected to an offshore account that no one but you and I can touch, and there's enough there for you to live more than comfortably for the rest of your life."

"And what about you? How will you live?" She turns the card in her hands, staring at it in the firelight.

I shrug. "The same way I've been living, just in a different country. I have the ticket to get me there, and that's all I really need. You needed the money."

She shakes her head and hands the card to me. "No, I needed more than that. I just didn't realize it until right now."

"What do you mean?"

"You, Grey. I need you." She turns to face me. "We've only known each other for a few weeks, but I need you. You've given me someone to come home to each day, and you've given me hope. That's something I haven't had since I was a little girl. But I can't have you."

"What are you talking about?" I pull her against my chest and hold her. "I just invited you to run away with me. That wasn't out of politeness. I want you with me too."

She pulls away and holds me at arm's length, then pushes the passports into my hands as well. "No. You want your wife, and I'll never be her."

As she turns and walks toward the house, my stomach drops into my feet. I stuff the passports into my pocket, and my hand collides with the mask. Closing my eyes, I grip the fabric and listen as the door to the house clicks shut behind Briar.

She's right. How can she want to be with me when I've never given her a chance to be with *me*? Every intimate moment we've shared has been facilitated by a middleman: this mask.

I grit my teeth and toss the mask into the fire before rushing into the house.

Briar stands in the kitchen beside the coffeemaker. Her auburn hair slides off of her shoulder as she turns to look at me. I step forward and take her upper arms into my hands again, but I won't release her this time. I don't care how much she struggles. She has to hear me.

"I want you, Briar. Without the mask. I don't want a barrier between us anymore, and after I fuck you, I want you to promise that you'll never hurt yourself. Ever. And then I want you to promise that you'll come with me."

"Let go. You're hurting me," she says as she struggles, but I don't release her.

"No. Not until you listen to me. I'll never be able to let go of the grief I feel for the life I once had, but when I found that note—" My throat closes off, and I can't continue. But I have to. "The wound had begun to close, and the same person who stitched me up had wrenched me open again. When I walked into this house, I had every intention of putting the card on the table and leaving without any fanfare, but I couldn't. Not without asking you to come with me."

She relaxes in my grip and looks at the floor. "Grey, it was fun while it lasted, but—"

I grab her hand and place it against my jeans. "I'm not wearing the mask, little psycho. I don't need it."

Her grip firms around my erection, and for a moment, I fear my cock will panic and recede inside my body. Instead, a rush of pleasure ratchets my spine straight, and I suck in a breath.

"I want you to touch me like that," I whisper. "I want to fuck you without the mask, and then I want to sleep until we need to catch that plane. That's all I want. Not the money. Not the old life. Just you."

She bites her lip and looks up at me. "Then take me."

I step into her and press my mouth to hers. Without any hesitation, I devour her and inhale her every breath. Her nipples pebbles against my palms as I touch her breasts. White heat pulses between my legs, and I want to give her every hardened inch of myself.

Gripping the hem of her shirt, I step back and pull it over her head, wanting to see every glimpse of her bare skin. She tries to cover herself, but I move her hands.

"You want me without the mask, and I want to see you. All of you. I want to touch and commit every inch of your perfect body to memory. Let me see you, Briar."

Instead of simply lowering her hands, she takes a deep breath and removes her pants, then her bra and underwear. Under my scrutinizing gaze, she strips until she's bare.

Raised scars crisscross her body. I've felt these marks,

but I always figured they were stretch marks and she was embarrassed. This is so much worse. These marks weren't caused by a natural occurrence. Whatever happened to Briar, I'm not sure it was natural at all. Nor was it consensual.

I get on my knees in front of her and pull her body closer. With my hands around her thigh, I place gentle kisses on the scars near my fingers. I turn her body, replacing every painful bit of abuse with kindness and attention.

"You're beautiful. Your scars are part of that beauty, little psycho. They're proof that you walked through hell and came out on the other side." I kiss a long, thick area of raised skin on her ass. I can't imagine what it must have been like, trying to sit down at work with a wound like this after enduring abuse to the point that it caused you to lose your pregnancy. "Never hide your body from me again."

I rise behind her and place my hands on either side of her on the counter, boxing her in. Her full ass presses against my cock. I reach up and ease her auburn hair over her shoulder so that I can see her face.

"Promise me, Briar."

She offers a nervous laugh. "I hate making promises, but that seems to be all you want tonight."

I position her hands on the counter, then begin unfastening my belt. When she tries to turn around, I stop her.

"Hold that counter, and don't let go," I say. I hurry and finish undressing.

When I step behind her again, my bare skin meets hers, and she sucks in a breath. I press my palm on her lower back, then glide toward the back of her neck. My fingertips drive into her hair, and I snatch back her head. As a small whimper leaves her throat, my cock jumps against her ass.

"You wanted all of me, so that's what you'll get, but I expect something in return. I want all of you, too. And if you're going to be mine, I want to know that you'll protect what's mine. Do you understand what I'm asking you?"

She nods her head.

"Good girl. Now grip that counter, and don't let go until I say you can."

I line up behind her as she braces herself, and the moment I sink inside, we both let out a groan. It's a feeling we didn't think we'd have the chance to experience again, and that makes it so much more intense now.

Another whimper sneaks out of her when I drive my hips forward and push her against the counter, but I told her to brace herself. I don't plan to go easy on her. She seems to get the memo, and she pushes back against me on the next thrust.

We communicate without words in a game of push and pull. Within minutes, her thighs begin to shake, and I'm too close to my edge as well. I pull out of her and sit in a chair.

"Ride me, little psycho. Fuck me until you force the come out of me. Take it. Take everything you deserve."

She turns and takes a few steps forward so that she can straddle me. Her left arm goes around my neck, and her right hand slips between us. She firms her grip on my cock, then pushes me inside her. I lean forward and moan against her shoulder. She feels like heaven.

Her tempo starts slow. With my size, this position can be a bit uncomfortable, but she's working herself up to it. She rises and drops with each scoop of her hips, and she's so focused. I look up and watch as her head tips back and she moans. Leaning forward, I pull her nipple into my mouth and suck.

"Oh, fuck," she whispers. "Just like that, but suck a little harder."

She picks up speed, coming down a little harder at the end of each scoop of her hips. I release her breast and look between us, watching the place where we join. Her swollen clit grinds against my pelvis, and my cock gleams with the proof of how good it feels to her.

Fuck, it feels good to me too, and if she keeps this up, I'm going to fill her.

I release her breast from my mouth and swap to using my hands. "Come for me, little psycho. Use me until you get what you need. Just like that."

She leans forward, gripping me and the chair as she chases her orgasm at a breakneck speed. Her hips pump like a machine, and she's milking both of us of every ounce of pleasure. Just when I'm not sure I can hold out any longer, she loses herself.

"Fuck, I'm coming! I'm fucking coming!" she screams, followed by a beautifully inhuman groan. Her thighs tense and release, tense and release, and there's no rhyme or reason to her tempo now. An intense orgasm has taken control, and it's taking me down with it.

Her perfect pussy squeezes my dick in time with her heartbeat. My arms wind around her waist, and I press my face against her chest as I fill her completely. A mixture of our come slides down my shaft and saturates my balls, but I don't care. As this unhinged psycho leans back and looks down at me, I don't know that I'll ever care about anything else again.

Besides her.

"So you'll come with me?" I whisper up at her as she looks into my eyes.

She smirks. "I just did."

"You know what I meant."

With a sigh, she relaxes forward and rests her head on mine. "Yes, Grey. I'm coming with you."

As I hold her against me, everything feels right again. If we can just make it onto that plane together, life might actually feel right forever.

Chapter Eighteen

Grey

With a giggle, she hurries off to the bathroom to clean up as I gather my clothes. We don't have a lot of time to pack before we have to take off, but I don't exactly have anything to pack anyway. That's all right. With all the money we have, we can both start over if we want to.

And I think that's exactly what we both want.

After dressing, I place the two passports and the bank card on the bedside table, then flop onto the bed. Briar joins me a few minutes later. She lies down beside me and snuggles against my chest.

"Can we get a dog?" she asks through a yawn. "When we get settled in Russia, I mean. I've always wanted a dog."

I smile and play with her hair. "Absolutely. What are you thinking? Something big and mean?"

"No, something small and cute."

I lean forward to kiss the top of her head. "Well, then I guess we'll have to get two dogs. Something big and mean for me and something small and cute for you."

That's when we hear the car door shut outside.

Briar and I sit up, but I motion for her to stay on the bed as I stand and walk toward the window. Without placing my silhouette within the curtain's frame, I peek through the small slit in the side and solidify our worst fears. A single cop car sits outside, and its lone officer is walking toward the front door.

I creep back to the bed. "It's a cop," I whisper. "He's probably stopping by to check out that lead again."

"About your car?"

I nod. "Just play it cool, little psycho. He'll leave, just like they did last time."

She blows out a breath and grabs her robe from the back of her bedroom door. The officer knocks as she's tying the silk belt around her waist.

"Just a moment!" Briar yells. "I'm not decent!"

"Good girl." I squeeze her shoulder. "I'll be in the hall closet, right near the door, so if he wants to take a look around, just steer him away from there at first. I'll slip outside and hide in the woods until the coast is clear."

She nods and licks her lips, then starts toward the front of the house. I spin on my heel to grab the passports and the bank card on the off chance that the officer asks to look around. I hurry to catch up, then tuck myself into the closet before she opens the door. Since I can't see anything, I close my eyes and listen.

The door creaks open, and Briar clears her throat. "Hello, officer. I've already told you I haven't seen the car."

That's not exactly playing it cool, but I can't blame her for jumping straight to that. She's in a very tough position, and I'm merely hiding in a closet.

"Oh, of course, ma'am, but would you mind if I have a look around your property? I know it's been a few weeks, but if he stashed his vehicle somewhere on your land, that would at least give us some kind of lead."

"My land?" The floor creaks as Briar adjusts her weight. "Like, you want to go tromping through my woods?"

"Yes, if that isn't too much of a bother."

"Well, it kind of is. I was just settling in for bed, and I won't sleep a wink if I think some murderer has been living in the woods. Maybe you should check the house first."

She's trying to give me a chance to get out, but in doing so, she's tightening the noose around her own neck. If they stay long enough to check the woods, they'll eventually discover the body tucked away in the forest. And it would be all my fault. Briar killed him, but I drew the flies to his corpse when I picked her driveway.

The voices and footsteps fade as Briar leads the policeman into the house. I catch the word "basement," followed by the familiar creak of the basement door. Then everything goes silent.

A cold sweat slicks my forehead as I prepare to exit the closet and make a break for the front door. I can only hope Briar takes my advice and plays it cool. The last thing we need is for her to panic and chain the officer in her sex dungeon.

I open the door and slip out of the house, holding my breath the entire way. My initial plan is to run to the woods and do something with Sid's body, but then I see the cop car. The computers inside their vehicles hold far too much information for me to just pass on by, especially when that information might pertain to me.

On silent feet, I hurry to the passenger side. Most cop cars also come equipped with cameras that film inside and outside the car whenever an officer turns on his body cam. Because that cop is inside a residence with a potential witness, I can almost guarantee his camera is on, which means the car cameras are as well. Thankfully, the car's nose is pointed at an angle, aimed away from the front door. When he watches the footage tomorrow, he might see movement or shadow, but he'll have no evidence of my existence.

I lean in through the open door, careful to keep most of my weight out of the car. Any shift in the camera's angle might alert them to the fact that I was snooping through their things. The computer monitor rests within a swivel arm attached to the dash. It's currently aimed toward the steering wheel, so I reach forward and twist it to face me. The words that stare back at me aren't what I expect to see. I anticipated information about my case, but the cop wasn't here for me at all.

He's here for a welfare check on Sid Williams.

The blood drains from my face. Briar has no idea, and she may be incriminating herself at this very moment. I have to do something, and fucking fast.

I ease out of the car and hurry around the side of the house, but I don't know why I'm being so sneaky. The plan formulating in my mind ends with me leading the police on a chase to draw them away from Briar, allowing her to escape.

Throwing myself onto the sword couldn't save my wife, but it might save Briar.

I drop to my stomach in front of the small window, then shimmy forward on my abdomen. The cop's back faces the window, and Briar faces him. I push my hand in front of the glass and wiggle my fingers, hoping against hope that Briar sees me.

Her eyebrows rise, and she looks me in the eye. Now what? How the fuck do I communicate that I need to get her upstairs so that I can speak to her?

I point at the cop, then point down. I point to Briar, then point up.

She looks at the cop and nods at whatever he's saying. After a few more nods and a bright smile, she says something else and points upstairs. The cop goes to follow her, but she shakes her head, says a few more words, and heads up the steps. He stays put.

Without a moment to spare, I scramble to my feet and rush toward the front of the house, but I stop at the corner. As soon as Briar pokes her head outside, I get her attention with a low-pitched whistle. She scurries toward me.

"What the fuck are you thinking? Why aren't you hiding in the woods?" she whispers. "I told him I needed to use the bathroom, so we don't have a lot of time to fucking chat."

I reach into my pocket and pull the bank card and Briar's passport from inside. I shove them into her hands, then tighten my fists over hers so that she can't give them back. "When you arrive at the airport in Russia—"

"Grey, no. I'm not leaving without you."

My grip tightens. "When you arrive at the airport, look for the man with a sign for the Robinsons. Go with him. He'll take you to the village. I'll join you as soon as I can."

"We don't have to split up. He'll leave when he's done looking through the house. I've already thought about it. When he finishes up in the—"

"He isn't here for me, Briar. He's here for you."

Her mouth closes, and her throat clicks as she swallows. The color drains from her face. "What?"

"I checked the cop car. There's a computer in there that sometimes says why they're out on a call, and this time, he's here for a welfare check."

"Well, yeah, to check on me in case—"

"For Sid Williams. They're here looking for your ex."

She closes her eyes, and a tear trails down her cheek. "What do we do?"

"When the cop is gone, you take my car and drive to the small airport outside of town. You know the rest."

"Why can't I take my car? And how will you meet me?"

I close my eyes and shake my head. "I can't go with you tonight, but I'll meet you in Russia as soon as I can. Our tickets are at the Gregario Airlines counter."

"Then I can't go tonight either. Why don't we meet—"

But then we both hear the footfalls coming up the creaking basement steps. I lean forward and kiss Briar for what is probably the final time, and then I step into the light.

"Little pig, little pig, are you looking for me?" I shout.

The cop's head whips upward, and his gaze meets mine. That's my cue.

I turn and race for the cop car, then hurl myself inside. The keys are still in the ignition, so I reach forward, turn them, and take off down the driveway. I consider running lights and sirens, but I need to put some space between myself and certain doom. Certain doom will probably still discover me, but at least I've kept Briar safe.

That thought consoles me as I step on the gas and race into the night.

Epilogue

Briar

A gentle breeze eases through my hair as I rock on the porch swing. Music plays from a radio aimed through the open window, but I don't understand a single lyric. Despite living in Russia for months, I've yet to learn the language.

The village is small, just like Grey said it would be. Most of the inhabitants speak English, and we consider this tiny patch of land to be our own Russian version of America. Just without all the nonsense.

And without all the stores on every corner, among other American conveniences.

I smile as I look at my crusty chicken coop and struggling garden. Since coming here, I've had to learn to fend for myself in ways I never imagined, but hey, I'm debt free. Most of the money still sits in the bank account as well. This new way of life is incredibly inexpensive.

It's also incredibly lonely.

I spend most of my day looking down the long dirt road

that leads onto our property. And it is *our* property. Until the American news agencies declare him dead, I will continue to think of everything as ours.

American news reaches this part of the world at a painfully slow pace, so it was weeks before I even learned what happened the night he took off in the cop car. After the officer commandeered my vehicle, Grey led them on a wild chase through backroads and forest country before finally abandoning the car and taking off on foot. They followed him as far as the Tamsen River Bridge, where he jumped into the frigid waters and never resurfaced.

But he will. If he had to swim the entire way to Russia, he'll resurface.

Nails clack on the wooden boards as our dog trots toward me with a massive stick in his mouth. I found him as a puppy shortly after I arrived, and he filled both requirements that Grey and I wanted in a dog. He's massive and mean, but he's also adorable. Especially when his droopy jowls lift in a smile as he carries a stick.

"Bring the prize to Mama, Meechi." I hold out my hand and giggle as he trots over and entices me into a game of keep away. "Give it here!"

He trots a few steps away, then stops and drops the stick. His floppy ears do their best to perk up as he looks toward the place where our driveway bends into the trees. I stop too. I hold my breath and watch that shadowy area, my brain screaming for me to start running, that Grey is just around the bend.

But then a rabbit hops across the road, and Demetri takes off after it.

"No! Bad dog!" I shout as I go after him, but it's no use. He'll never catch the rabbit, but I can't stop him from chasing it.

I halt beside the tree line and sigh as Demetri's tail disappears through the trees. Another breeze kicks up, and I rub my bare arms to stave off the slight chill. That's when I realize the goosebumps aren't from the breeze. It feels as if someone's watching me.

I lunge toward the massive stick that Demetri dropped, then spin around and wave the weapon toward whatever monster lurks behind me. Only . . . it isn't a monster. He's a few pounds lighter, and his eyes look so tired, but beneath the thick beard, I can't mistake the face looking back at me. The eyes haven't changed a bit.

"Grey?" I breathe. "Is it really you?"

He steps forward finally and takes me into his arms. "I'm sorry it took so long."

With shaking hands, I touch his face. I can't help it. I have dreamed of this moment so many times, and I want to be sure this isn't a dream too. But my fingers don't fade through him. When he leans down and presses his lips to mine, only then do I believe that this moment isn't another hopeful figment of my tired imagination.

"Where have you been? How did you get here?" I brush the hair out of his eyes because I don't want to spend another moment of my life without looking into them. "Have you been safe? Are you hurt anywhere?"

He tips his head back and laughs. "I've been in hiding, but I've been well. Just terribly, terribly lonely. Have you missed me as much as I've missed you?"

"I haven't thought about you a single time," I say with a smirk.

As he bends to kiss me again, the dog races past, nearly knocking us down.

"Meechi, leave the rabbit alone!" I shout.

Grey's eyebrow rises. "Meechi is . . . your dog?"

"When he's good, he's mine. When he's bad, he's yours. But he's always been ours in my mind."

"Ours." Grey's smirk shifts into a soft smile. "I like that."

He takes my hand, and we start toward the little house that is ours. The garden in the backyard is ours too. And this happiness. That's ours.

Maybe killing the head of a bank and murdering an abusive man weren't the right things to do, but sometimes even the bad guys get a happy ending when they kill the bad guys who are worse. That's how I sleep at night, anyway.

Grey releases my hand and starts up the porch steps. As he reaches the top, he grips the tall post that could use a new coat of paint, then looks back at me. "It's perfect, Briar. Our new life is everything I hoped it would be."

"How can you say that when you've been living it for all of ten seconds?" I laugh and turn toward the yard. "Wait until you have to chase a fox out of the chicken coop at three in the morning, then see how much you love it."

He shakes his head and looks out at our land. "You have no idea how much I've missed you, do you?"

I shrug and turn to face him. "Probably about as much as I've missed you."

"Then why don't we go inside and show each other just how much we've been missing?"

As curious as I am to learn about where he's been and how he finally arrived here, the need to have him inside me again is much stronger. I rush up the steps and enter his arms, and for the first time in my life, nothing is missing at all. That empty space in my chest is full, and I've never felt more complete.

"That might take all night," I say as I look into his eyes.

"It might take the rest of our lives," he says, then scoops me into his arms and carries me into the house.

Thank you for reading. If you enjoyed this book, please consider Lauren Biel's other offerings.

If you want to stay with light-gray books:
Sinners Retreat: Books2read.com/SinnersRetreat
Stranger Session: Books2read.com/StrangerSession
Her Fantasy: Books2read.com/HerFantasy
Last Mistake: Books2read.com/LastMistake
Protect Me: Books2read.com/ProtectMeNovella

If you're ready to dive into darker reads, make sure you check out the dark hitchhiker standalones in the Ride or Die romance series. These can be read in any order:

Hitched: Books2read.com/Hitched
Along for the Ride: Books2read.com/MFMHitchhiker
Driving my Obsession: Books2read.com/
DrivingmyObsession
Across State Lines: Books2read.com/AcrossStateLines
Don't Stop: Books2read.com/Dont-Stop

If you want to venture into the pitch-black side of things:
Captured: Books2read.com/Captured
Never Let Go: Books2read.com/NLG

Connect with Lauren

Don't miss a thing from Lauren Biel! Check out all of her books, social media connections, and other important information at Campsite.bio/LaurenBielAuthor and Lauren Biel.com

Acknowledgments

To my VIP gals (Jessie, Nikita, Lexi, Grace, and Kim): love you! Thank you for always helping me.

Thank you, Mr. Biel, for being you. I love you!

Brooke, my editor, you're the greatest.

Thank you to my valued Patrons. Your contribution helped make this book happen:

Tammy, Curvy Pear, Kim R, Leslie R, Janelle, Megan L, Laura F, Brianna B, Ashley S, Nikkie B, Rebecca C, Kaat, Emily S, Kimberly G, Bunny, A.Reads, Samantha O, Danielle N, CJ, Sara M, Harley B, Jenn C, Heather M, Bonnie F, Pyro, Iris, Marguerite, Courtney, PaigeeBear, Sarah S, Tiffany M, Tara H, Vikki S, Amanda T, Suzy A, Andie J, Lisa W, Court's Bookshelf, Nicholetta88, Emily S, Sheena E, Queen Ilmaree, SerenaLorraine, Iesha E, April-Coats, Jasmine K, Heather S, Lizzie Borden, Jennifer S, Just Jen Here, Mikasa_Kuchiki, Jada W, Briyanna M, Shannan T, Heather C, Jesi D, Charmaine B, Michelle, Christy P, Melissa, Dani C, Callie K, Kayla T, Arnica S, Cassi K, Gumdrop, Maxine T, Amanda C, Barrie, Alexandria R, Leeat S, Leslie W, Kayla M, Marisa K, Smitty, Brooke, Ashley P, Mandy G, Anna S, Shelby F, Tiannah B, Sharee

S, Courtney P, Kristiana B, Vero A, Chelle, Sara S, Samantha R, Jessica G, Kimberly S, StjoReads, Tabitha F, JesStenger, Lindsey S, Laura T, Joanna, Nicole M, Eugenia M, Nineette W, BoneDaddyAshe, Kimberly B

Also by Lauren Biel

To view Lauren Biel's complete list of books, visit: https://laurenbiel.com/laurenbielbooks/

About the Author

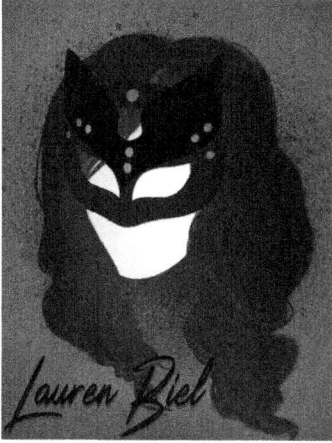

Lauren Biel is the author of many dark romance books, with several more titles in the works. When she's not working, she's writing. When she's not writing, she's spending time with her husband, her friends, or her pets. You might also find her on a horseback trail ride or sitting beside a waterfall in Upstate New York. When reading her work, expect the unexpected. To be the first to know about her upcoming titles, please visit www.LaurenBiel.com.

Printed in Great Britain
by Amazon